# A GATHERING OF WOLVES

*Also by Michael Hammonds*

CONCERNING THE DEATH OF CHARLIE BOWMAN
AMONG THE HUNTED
ONE TO RIDE THE RIVER WITH

# A GATHERING OF WOLVES

### MICHAEL HAMMONDS

DOUBLEDAY & COMPANY, INC.

GARDEN CITY, NEW YORK

1975

Athens Regional Library
Athens, Georgia

All of the characters in this book
are fictitious, and any resemblance
to actual persons, living or dead,
is purely coincidental.

Library of Congress Cataloging in Publication Data

Hammonds, Michael.
   A gathering of wolves.

   I. Title.
PZ4.H2265Gat  [PS3558.A454] 813'.5'4
ISBN 0–385–09690–9
Library of Congress Catalog Card Number 74–33741

*First Edition*

Copyright © 1975 by Michael Hammonds
All Rights Reserved
Printed in the United States of America

*For my Mother and Father*
*two of my best friends*

188462

# A GATHERING OF WOLVES

# ONE

Riding hard, the five men topped the ridge above the town in the dark morning light.

The man in the lead, Walt Canfield, held up his hand for them to halt.

"Take a rest," he told them, then nudged his horse on down the slope another ten feet and dismounted.

A tall, angular man, he wore an old army campaign hat tipped slightly forward on his head. The flat brim and peaked crown of the hat intensified the sharpness of his face and the concentration in his gaze as he crouched down beside his horse, his eyes moving to the road leading into town from the west. Waiting.

Above him, the men's voices mixed with shadow. He was about to tell them to be quiet when another sound drew his attention back to the road.

Sharp. Puncturing the still black air. Canfield smiled. It was the clatter of a horseless carriage engine.

Standing up slowly, he strained to see, then spotted the two small lights moving across the flats, down the road toward town.

"Gage," he called back over his shoulder.

A figure separated from the others and came down the slope.

Canfield glanced around as the massive shadow stopped beside him. Canfield wondered sometimes how anybody could manage shoulders that big. Even under his duster Phil Gage looked like he could break a bull's back.

"Ballard and the girl?" the big man asked.

Canfield nodded. "I'm goin' down to see that she gets on that mail coach," he said.

"Just her and that old man, the hotel clerk said yesterday," Gage recalled.

"I know," Canfield nodded. "I'm just gonna make sure. You take 'em on to the ravine."

Gage's eyes came around and he smiled slightly. "You makin' me the lieutenant?"

Canfield returned his smile wanly. "Only one qualified," he said, and glanced up the slope, his eyes surveying the other men.

Rem Sidy, the oldest, a grizzle-bearded man, was complaining about his leg. He was always complaining about something. Next to him was Jed Logan. Small, thin-faced, and quiet. The third, Howie Taylor, was the youngest. Looked like he should be in a classroom somewhere learning how to spell.

"Damn," Canfield sighed, shaking his head. "Not a soldier in the bunch," and turning, he mounted his horse and rode back up to Taylor.

"Howie."

The boy looked up. "Yessir."

"Time you were movin' too."

The boy nodded. "Yessir," he said. Hurrying to his feet and mounting up, he rode out along the ridge and around the town.

"Sure wish I had me that contraption of Ballard's." Rem Sidy nodded toward the moving lights. "Go back to Mexico in style."

Canfield turned his horse down the slope. "His daughter's enough for now," he said, and spurred the animal toward town.

The sputter of the horseless carriage engine pulled Jake Hooker's eyes up from the boot he was tugging on. Hesitating on the hotel bed where he sat, he listened to the carriage clamor between the old buildings of the small New Mexico town and squeal to a halt below him.

Frowning, he stamped the boot the rest of the way on, and standing, pushing his long graying hair back from his bearded face, he ambled across the hotel room to the window, looking down into the street.

The horseless carriage was parked directly beneath him, still alive and shaking. Mint new and shiny. Jake didn't know its name. He didn't care to. A 1913 something. Nothing more than a wagon with an engine and a guide bar; it looked clumsy and ridiculous, like a skinny man jumping a rail fence. All asses and elbows. Even the two people on it—a young woman and a heavy-set man—looked out of place. Perched. Like they might topple any second. The girl was still holding on after the engine chugged into silence and the man climbed down and came around to help her.

Jake's frown deepened, and turning back into the room, he lifted his eyes and caught the drift of mist through the mountains to the south. The peaks were dark. White, gray-black, and blue. Nearly breathing.

A knot of regret twisted in his throat. He had spent most of his life in mountains like those. He was sorry to be leaving them. But it had to be done.

A knock at the door pulled his gaze back into the room.

"Come in, Pike," he said, and turned to the chair beside the bed. There was a shirt, hat, and coat hanging on it, a traveling bag beside it. All were new.

Jake picked up the shirt as the door burst open and Pike Hungerford stalked into the room. Tall, he was dressed in buckskins that smelled of wood smoke. A half-angry frown weighted his face.

He pointed to the window. "What the hell's all the commotion out there?"

Jake grinned. "Devil come for you, Pike," he said, buttoning his shirt.

"Have to get in line," the buckskinned man grumbled,

and strode to the window, looking down as Jake pushed the shirt into his pants.

Pike shook his head grimly. "How can somethin' that ugly shine that much?"

"Ain't easy," Jake frowned.

"What the hell they call it, again? Remember that fella down in the bar said it was the only one in southern New Mexico."

"Horseless carriage."

"Yeah," Pike nodded, and turned back into the room, looking to Jake as he stretched into his new coat. Pike shook his head disgustedly, his eyes moving up and down.

"You look terrible," he concluded.

"Thanks, Pike."

"Even smell funny."

Jake looked away. "That's the bath," he said.

Pike's eyes came up and he smiled. "What the hell'd you do that for? Ain't finally thinkin' of somebody else are you?"

"Felt like it," Jake answered tersely.

Shrugging, Pike scratched his leathers. "Ain't no reason you gotta take that coach to the railhead, you know. We could always ride it. Maybe head up around Taos. Old Ef Tyne is—"

Jake shook his head. "Taos is further'n I need to go. And a waste of time. Catch the train from Albuquerque. Be in California in a week or so."

Pike nodded wearily. "You pretty well set on this I ta' it?"

"Yeah," Jake frowned.

"Australia," Pike said distastefully. "That the name of place?"

From his dresser, Jake picked up a handful of coins and a knife in its scabbard.

"That's it," he nodded, slipping the coins into his pocket. He undid his belt and strung the knife on it.

"Figger you're gonna need that?" Pike pointed at the knife.

Jake glanced down at the knife and buckled his belt. "Some habits die hard. Never felt right without one."

"Know the feelin'," Pike nodded, then pointed at Jake's coat. "You still carryin' that paper money?"

Jake patted his chest. "Right here."

Pike shook his head ruefully. "Won't listen to me about nothin' will you? Paper money ain't no good."

"I'd have a hellava time carryin' around three thousand in gold," he said, picking up his hat and putting it on.

Pike shrugged. "Guess so," he allowed; then slapping Jake on the shoulder, he picked up his bag from the foot of the bed. "Well, if you're bound to do this thing, we might as well get some breakfast, then put you on that stage good and drunk."

They started out the door.

"Course I ain't too hungry this mornin'," Pike went on as they descended the stairs. "Maybe six, eight eggs, dozen biscuits, steak, gravy. . . ."

Standing on the hotel porch, Addie Ballard unbuttoned her duster. She watched her father unloading her bags from the horseless carriage for a moment, then glanced up and down the empty street.

"Will it be here soon?" she asked, an anxious irritation edging her voice.

Her father paused, looking up at her. "What? The coach? Yeah. Not long," he nodded, and lifted another bag to the porch.

Still half-looking up the street, she turned, slipping the duster off, and looked into the window of the hotel to straighten her new dress and hat.

The glass echoed a girl of sixteen. Tall, fine-boned, well dressed, and plain-faced.

Her eyes hovered on the reflection of her face for a moment. No matter how many times she looked at it, she expected it to be different the next time. It wasn't. Still too broad. Too flat.

Funny, she frowned. The new clothes and the styling of her blond hair were meant to help, but they just seemed to make her more homely by contrast.

Behind her, her father said something.

She turned back to him. "What?" she nearly snapped.

"That's the bags," he repeated, and nodded at the duster in her hand. "I'll put that back."

"Oh," she said, remembering it, and handed it to him.

Taking the duster, he laid it over the seat; then unbuttoning his own, he revealed an immaculate suit beneath. Smoothing the coat, his eyes wandered over the buildings and he stood in an uncomfortable silence.

Across the street, the door of the General Store and Post Office opened and a small man wearing an apron rolled a barrel of brooms out to hold the door open.

"Mornin', Herb," Ballard called.

The storekeeper looked up. "Mr. Ballard," he nodded. "Little early for mail, yet."

Ballard shook his head. "Waitin' for the coach. Daughter's goin' back to school."

Herb looked to her. "Mornin', Miss Addie."

"Mr. Green."

"Could get it for you," the storekeeper offered. "Take a minute, but I could—"

Ballard shook his head again. "No. I'll be over in a bit. See my daughter off."

The storekeeper shrugged. "Whatever you want, Mr. Ballard. Nice to see you 'gin, Miss Addie." He gave her a mandatory grin and went back inside.

The silence drifted between Addie and her father again.

"There's no need for you to wait," she finally said.

"I don't mind," her father said, and cleared his throat. "Guess you'll be glad to be back."

Addie frowned, her hands tightened on her purse. "There's no need to make polite conversation either, Papa."

Linus Ballard looked up at her for a long moment, then tried to smile it away. "Thought that was what I sent you to school for. To learn to make polite conversation."

"And play the piano and sew." She continued his line of thought through tight lips.

Her father stiffened. "You make it sound like somethin' terrible. When your mama passed on, I just wanted—

"You just wanted something to overcome a plain face in finding a husband."

"Now, Addie—"

"Oh hell, Papa, be honest about it. Having a daughter who'll most certainly be an old-maid is more than your pride can bear."

Her father's eyes narrowed in anger. "Don't you lecture me on honesty, young lady. Honesty," he said sourly. "You swear like that around the teachers?"

The girl swallowed. "If I feel like it."

Ballard's eyes softened, knowing she was lying, and he nodded. "You thought about what you're gonna do after next year when you graduate?"

The girl's eyes fell. "No," she said.

"You can't stay there the rest of your life, you know."

Her eyes came up. "There are other schools. College."

Ballard nodded. "Yeah," he acknowledged. "There are other schools."

The silence settled between them again. A dog barked, mixing with early morning rustlings. The blacksmith down the street opening his doors. The liveryman putting horses out in the corral. Soft hoof rattles up the street as a man rode in following the tire tracks Addie and her father had made earlier.

"What time is it?" Addie asked.

Ballard slipped his watch from his vest pocket. "Ten till seven," he answered, and replaced the watch. His eyes lingered on her for a moment, and he started to say something; giving it up, he ambled into the dusty street, pausing, watching the rider approach and go by down the street.

The rider was a tall man, shadowed by the early light. Wearing an old army campaign hat. Addie felt his eyes pass over her, then ease away beneath the brim of the hat.

Ballard looked at the sky. "Nice day for travelin'," he nodded. "Little hot, maybe." He walked back to the porch. "Maybe . . . maybe we can make a trip next summer," he offered. "Down to Mexico. Monterrey."

"Maybe," she allowed. "I don't know, Papa."

Ballard nodded. "All that trouble they're havin' down there with Villa should be done by then. Course," he smiled, "all that trouble's bringing me a lot of money. Folks sellin' off their cattle cheap, just want to get out."

Her eyes hardened. "Yes, that is lucky for you."

Ballard's eyes came up, the muscles in his jaws cording, then easing. "Hell," he sighed. "I don't want to get into it with you again. You think we could have a cup of coffee without bitin' at each other?"

Frowning, Addie nodded. "I suppose," she said, and turning, she noticed the man in the campaign hat again looking at them.

She hesitated and he looked away.

"Papa?" Addie nodded toward the man. "Do you know him?"

Ballard looked toward the man as he dismounted. "No, I don't think so. Why?"

"Nothing," she shrugged, and went on into the hotel.

At the hitching rack, Canfield pulled his eyes away from Ballard and his daughter and stepped down from the saddle.

Looping the reins around the rack, he mounted the porch and pushed through the swinging door into the Cattleman's Bar.

It was dim inside, like some of the night had been forgotten. Squinting, Canfield was able to make out a man behind the bar. Gaunt. Pale, a hangover thickening his movements. Something else forgotten by darkness.

The barkeep looked up.

"Yeah?"

"Coffee," Canfield said.

The barkeep frowned. "Don't make much on coffee. How 'bout something to put hair on you?"

"Little early."

"Meal then?"

Canfield shook his head. "Coffee," he said quietly.

Shrugging his surrender, the pale barkeep put a cup on the counter. "On the Acme," he pointed at the stove by the window. "It's free."

Nodding and taking the cup, Canfield walked back to the stove, poured himself some coffee, then stepped to the table in front of the window and sat down.

Through the dirty glass, he could see the hotel porch again.

Leaning back in his chair, he sipped his coffee and waited.

# TWO

Pike Hungerford shook his head. Leaning on the bar, Jake smiled.

This would be the seventh or eighth time this morning alone Pike was going to tell him he was making a mistake.

"You're makin' a mistake," Pike grumbled, and Jake's smile pushed to laughter.

Turning to the bar, Jake sipped his whiskey. "You've mentioned it before," he nodded.

"Well, you might try listenin' for once," Pike snapped half angrily, then shook his head. "No," he frowned. "Why should you start now?"

"You're gettin' testy in your old age."

Pike looked at him. "I ain't that much older'n you are." He downed his whiskey and poured another. "Least I don't think I am. Lost track back there somewhere."

Jake smiled and nodded. "Thought about where you're gonna winter, yet?"

"Been considerin' the Wind Rivers. Figured I'd see who's still there."

"Should be a good winter. No trouble with the Crow no more."

"No," Pike frowned regretfully. "Not much any more. 'Fraid we killed most of 'em off. And the government stuck 'em on them passels of ground. Too bad—"

"Yeah," Jake agreed. "But it may keep you from gettin' your hair lifted."

"Hell," Pike grumbled. "Don't need the goddamn government to keep my hair for me. Outrun the Crow—and practically ever'body else—many a time." He turned to Jake.

"You recollect that time you and me come down that canyon on Mad Woman Creek? Right into that camp of Crow!" He hooted laughter, slapping the bar. "Had the damnedest look on their faces, sleep still in their eyes, and here come we two boys like a couple of innocents."

"Like to have seen our faces," Jake interjected, grinning. "Hell, I couldn't've been fifteen—"

"How long we run from 'em?"

"Day or two."

"Nearer three," Pike guessed.

Jake nodded. "Likely."

Pike downed his drink and poured another. "Damn." He cocked his head, smiling. "They give us a good run," he remembered admiringly.

"Yeah," Jake agreed.

From beyond the swinging doors, the rattle of horses approaching webbed the dim room. They halted in front of the hotel.

Jake glanced around at the door. "Looks like I'm about to head out," he said, and downed his drink. Placing the glass back on the bar, he reached down and picked up his bag, then ambled to the door and into the sunlight.

The coach stood before him. More shadow in the early light than anything else. Waiting.

Jake swallowed. "Hello," he called to the driver, and tossed up his bag.

"Jake—" Pike said.

Jake looked at him and smiled. "You gonna tell me I'm makin' a mistake again?"

Pike's old face rumbled in a reluctant grin. "Could, but I always suspected you should be drilled for a hollow horn." The smile faded. "I never been one to curious into another man's cache, you know that. Just that you're fifty-five years old, Jake. What the hell you gonna do in this Australia?"

"Find some land," Jake answered quietly. "Some without fences."

"Hell," Pike growled. "There's plenty of land here. What about that valley you always talked about in Flathead country?"

Jake blinked, his face hardening suddenly. "There's fences in it," he said.

"Fences," Pike said, following him. "Hell, I didn't know anybody was up in there."

Jake nodded. "Came down out of the Flatheads along the divide one spring couple years ago. Barbed wire all over the place."

Pike frowned, nodding slowly. "I know how you was fond of that place, Jake. Talked about it for a lot of years."

"That's the trouble," Jake turned. "I talked too long. Waited too long."

"There's other places—"

"No," Jake shook his head. "This country's fillin' up. Australia's new. Hardly no people at all—"

Pike nodded knowingly. "That's it ain't it? People again." He frowned. "I never seen a man so bent on bein' lonesome, Jake." His eyes lifted to Jake's face, softening slightly. "Forty years I've knowed you, and you still ain't let go of what happened back in Ohio."

Jake's eyes pulled up, widening with sudden anger. "Pike," he snapped, then swallowed, forcing control through his voice. "What happened ain't none of your concern."

"That's probably true enough," Pike allowed. "But I always sorta liked you, Jake, ever since I picked you up off the bank of the Missouri." He frowned, shaking his head. "You ever think that them that killed your family's most like dead now themselves?"

Jake's mouth tightened. "A whole town, Pike? I hope so," he nodded.

"All right." Pike sighed his surrender. "I had my say I reckon. But folks'll be comin' to Australia too. You can't outrun 'em."

"Have up till now," Jake nodded. "Maybe I can a while longer—"

Behind them, the driver shouted, "This here mail coach is goin' to the railhead. Anybody wants a ride, better be on in two minutes flat."

Jake glanced up at the coach, then back at Pike.

"Watch your hair," he said.

Pike nodded, "Watch yours. You know my run in the Wind Rivers," he said; then turning, he walked abruptly away.

Jake watched him stride around the coach horses and across the street to the livery.

"So long, Pike," he said, and climbed into the coach.

At the driver's call, Addie Ballard's eyes jerked up.

"I didn't hear them come in," she said, and hurriedly gathered in her purse and got up from the table.

"Take your time," her father said, putting a coin on the table, but she was already headed for the door.

Frowning, Ballard followed her. As he came out on the porch, he tapped the shotgun rider on the shoulder. A short, wiry man, he turned and peered up at Ballard. "Yeah?"

"Her bags are there," Addie's father said, pointing out the luggage down the walk.

"I don't—" the shotgun rider began, then recognition blinked through his eyes. "Oh, right, Mr. Ballard," and he hurried down the walk.

Addie frowned as her father turned back to her.

"I'd better get aboard," she said.

Ballard glanced at the shotgun rider picking up the bags, then brought his eyes back to his daughter. "You . . . write."

"All right," she nodded, turning quickly to the coach, and stepping through the door and inside.

"See you Christmas," he said.

"That's it," the shotgun rider yelled, and coming by the door, he climbed aboard.

"Good-by," Ballard said.

And suddenly the coach was moving. Rushing forward

with the pull of the horses. Addie saw her father easing
back and away. She started to raise her hand but he was
already turning, stepping down from the sidewalk. Her
hand drifted back to her lap, and she settled back into the
seat.

Thank God, she thought, closing her eyes. Thank God
she was going back. Back to where it was safe.

As the coach passed Walt Canfield he put his coffee cup
down and sat forward in the chair he had taken in the
saloon. He watched the coach clamor out of town, then
shifted his gaze to Linus Ballard crossing the street to the
General Store and Post Office.

Ballard went inside and Canfield stood up. Lifting a cigar
from his shirt pocket, he bit off the end and lit it.

Two minutes later Ballard came back out the door of the
General Store and Post Office carrying a packet of mail.

Canfield's eyes stayed on Ballard until he had cranked
the horseless carriage to sputtering life, mounted the seat,
and turned the machine back out of town.

Nodding, Canfield stood up from the table.

"Come back," he heard the barkeep offer wearily as he
went out the door.

Crossing the walk, he ambled across the street and into
the General Store.

Behind the counter, the storekeeper turned toward him.
A small man with thinning brown hair, he nodded to Canfield.

"Morning," he smiled. A business smile. A smile for
strangers.

"Morning," Canfield nodded back. "Hopin' to catch Linus
Ballard 'fore he got his mail. Understand he might be in
this mornin'."

"Not only this mornin'. Ever' mornin', regular as clock-
work," the storekeeper nodded. "You just missed him."

"Did I? Damn," Canfield frowned.

"Likely catch him," the storekeeper said. "Ain't been gone a couple of minutes."

"No," Canfield shook his head, concerned. "'Fraid I ain't got the time." He paused, then looked up. "You say he comes in about this time regular—"

"Ever' day for the past twenty-two years. 'Cept Sunday. Galls Linus a little, I think, knowin' the government don't work on Sunday, even if he does."

"If I wrote him out a note, you think he'd get it in the mornin'?"

"Sure as the sun risin'," the storekeeper nodded.

The man grinned. "Can I borrow some paper from you? And a pencil?"

The storekeeper brought them, and Canfield flattened the paper on the counter. He was poising the pencil when he realized he had lost track of the date. He frowned. He didn't usually do things like that.

He looked up at the storekeeper.

"What date is it?" he asked.

"Tuesday," the storekeeper answered. "The third," then added with a grin, "All day."

Canfield smiled thinly. "Yeah," he nodded and going back to the paper, he wrote:

"By the time you read this I'll have your daughter. If you don't believe me, check the stage stop or telegraph the railhead.

"Bring ten thousand dollars to Long's Meadow above Miller's Store. Be there Friday, the sixth. Come alone. Don't follow us and don't tell anybody what you're doing. You do and your daughter's dead."

# THREE

Settling back into the calf-leather seat, Jake tried again to relax and watch the country go by, but it was no use.

He glanced at the girl across from him and frowned.

He'd made a mistake traveling like this. He knew that now. It was just that he had been in a hurry to get moving and get to Australia. Going to California by horse would have taken him months. This way it would be about a week. And he had liked that idea, and still did. He wanted to get gone. It was just that this way he was going to have to put up with people.

Like this girl.

Somehow or another, he hadn't figured on this. Being trapped inside a small box with a stranger. And a female stranger at that.

He looked back out the window, watching the mountains slip away south, falling into the hot desert floor.

Since he'd come west he'd stayed away from other folks, living in the mountains, descending to the towns only when the need for supplies forced him to. He'd spent a lot of years up there. Just how many, he didn't really know.

He had never really been concerned with time that way. Not in numbers. Only seasons. When game was plentiful and when it was not.

He glanced at the girl again.

Now he was going to have to put up with people; he frowned, then touched the bulge of money in his coat pocket. But not for long, he thought. Not for long.

Still looking at the girl, he shifted on the seat uncomfortably. Her eyes came around, touching his, then moved away.

Jake shrugged. Just as well, he thought, then found himself easing another look at her, something about her eyes drawing him back.

She was a plain-faced youngster, but that something in her eyes held him for a moment. Whatever it was, it wasn't quite all there yet. Right now her eyes were a mixture of things. Anger, fear, and distance. Like a reflection . . .

Her gaze came back around, meeting his accidentally. For a second they stared at one another, and Jake felt like he'd just been caught peeking in a window.

He grinned, embarrassed, and because of the closeness of the coach, he felt obligated to say something.

"Goin' far?" was all he could think of.

"Santa Fe," she answered. "Back to school."

"School," Jake nodded. "What you learnin' to be?"

The girl shook her head. "No. It's not a school like that. It's a finishing school."

"Finishin' school?"

"It's a school where you learn about being a lady."

Jake nodded. "Sounds like someplace you go if you ain't finished yet."

The girl smiled without wanting to. "Yes it does," she said, trying to press the smile away, but not succeeding.

Jake liked her smile. It made him feel less uneasy and it softened her eyes, taking the guardedness out of them, making them pretty.

"Long way to go to school, Miss—"

"Ballard." She gave him her name before she thought. "Addie Ballard."

"Jake Hooker." His fingers touched the brim of his hat. "You like it there? School, I mean."

"Yes."

"Course, I guess it ain't like livin' at home."

Her eyes darkened. "I wouldn't know. I've lived at school for the past seven years."

Jake nodded, realizing he'd gone where he shouldn't have. "Well," he tried to get out of it, "some fella'll grab you up 'fore long and give you a place of your own."

Addie's eyes flared. "Mr. Hooker," she snapped, "contrary to popular belief a woman doesn't need a goddamned man to live. Many have done it without one. I've gotten by so far, I expect to in the future." Her eyes snapped back to the window.

Jake blinked.

"Well, miss," he smiled slowly, "guess I been duly told." He nodded, then added, "And if bluff'll get you by, you've got a head start."

Walt Canfield rode five miles out of town, then off the road along a low run of hills to the foot of a table rock and around it, then down the bank of an arroyo. He followed the arroyo for a hundred yards, then came around a sharp bend and the three men and their horses slipped into view.

Gage and Logan were sitting, leaning back up against a rock. A few feet away Rem Sidy was stretched out prone on the ground, his hat over his face.

Gage and Logan stood up as Canfield rode in; Sidy didn't stir.

Canfield dismounted, his eyes on the sleeping man.

"Get the horses," he told Logan.

Shrugging, Logan brushed past them.

Canfield's eyes moved to the man on the ground again.

"He dead?"

"Said he didn't sleep good," Gage answered.

"He never sleeps good," Canfield observed sourly. "'Cept when he's supposed to be doin' somethin' else. All he ever thinks about is the next drink, his bum leg, and that easy chair he wants to buy and put on a porch someplace."

"We all get old," Gage said.

"He ain't just old, he's stupid."

Gage's eyes narrowed. "What the hell you so mad about, Walt? I didn't know you better, I'd think you were jumpy."

Canfield looked at him, then smiled tightly. "Just that you and me are the only two ex-military in the bunch, I guess. The more military you've got, the more of an edge you have."

"You and your edge," Gage grinned. "You're the only man I ever knew that went into a whore house and looked for the back door first."

"Good tactics," Canfield shrugged, and his smile loosened a little. "Those were good boys we had down in Guatemala."

"Yeah," Gage agreed.

Canfield's eyes came up. "Heard you got shot up a while back down in the Sierra Madres. Got laid up with some farmers."

Gage's face darkened in memory. "Somethin' like that," he said.

Behind them, Logan approached with the horses, and Canfield's eyes returned to Sidy. "Time he was seein' the light of day. For the second time in six hours," he growled, and ambled out to the old man.

He stood over Sidy for a moment, then kicked his limp boot. Hard.

Sidy jerked up into a sitting position, sleep still puffing his eyes and old grizzled face.

"What the hell?" he barked.

"We're movin'," Canfield said.

Sidy scratched his gray bald scalp, and getting up, he raked the butt of his pistol across a small rock, dragging it from the holster, sending it clattering to the ground.

"And be careful with that," Canfield snapped. "I didn't bust my butt getting automatics for you just to foul up."

Sidy picked up the .45 and shoved it back in the holster. "Jesus," he grumbled, "think we was Regular Army or something."

Canfield pulled himself up into the saddle. "As far as you're concerned we are," he said. "Now let's go."

Canfield led his men cross country for three hours. A half an hour before noon, they came up a low twist of hills and reined in.

"Station's just over that rise," Canfield said, glancing around. "Where the hell's Taylor?"

"There." Gage pointed to a man riding from behind a knot of rocks a hundred yards away.

Spurring the horses out, they rode to him.

"Captain," he nodded as they approached, the eagerness bristling his voice and widening his eyes.

Canfield nodded in response, and glanced up the hill. "Let's take a look," he said, and they turned their horses up the incline, reining in on the crest.

Below them in the flat was a small adobe house, barn, and a large corral, with upwards of ten horses in it.

"Still just the one man?" Canfield asked.

Taylor nodded. "Just him."

"Jed," Canfield said, and the narrow-faced man looked up. "Go wide," he ordered him, and wordlessly Logan swung his horse out.

"The rest of us are goin' straight in," Canfield said, and eased his horse down the incline toward the station.

# FOUR

The stationman, Jim McCanless, came out of his main house and was started toward the corrals when he saw the riders coming down from the ridge.

Halting a moment, the squat little man's eyes followed them as they came down the slope and across the road.

Four of them, McCanless counted, and a knot began to gather in the pit of his stomach.

His eyes eased back toward the house. He could see the gleam of the metal of the rifle resting beside the door.

Turning, he started back across the yard toward the house. Maybe he was bein' foolish, he thought, but he didn't like a whole hellava lot of folks ridin' in when a stage was due.

The riders started around the point of the corral. Tall man in front, wearing a campaign hat.

"Mornin'," he called, halting McCanless.

McCanless' eyes moved back to him, then to the door again. It was over twenty feet away.

Pushing a smile through his face, McCanless looked up to greet the men.

"Mornin'," he called back. "What're you fellas doin' out this way?"

The man in the lead smiled back. "Not much really." He came across the yard. "Headin' up toward the Blue-water, hopin' to come across a little work—"

"Little late," McCanless said. "'Course you might have some luck." He glanced toward the house. "Welcome to some coffee if you like, just put it on."

The man in the campaign hat nodded. "That'd be agreeable, thank you," he said, and started easing down from the saddle.

"Get it for you," McCanless said, turning a little too quickly, walking toward the door and the rifle resting just inside it.

He rushed beneath the leaning shade porch, and was stepping inside the door when he felt a sudden flicker of movement behind him.

And the barrel of a gun cracked across the back of his head.

The coach crashed through a dry wash and up a small hill. Cresting it, the driver squinted and could make out the stage stop in front of him.

"McCanless'," he said to the shotgun rider next to him, then frowned. "Sonofabitch," he spat.

"What's wrong?" the shotgun rider asked.

"McCanless oughta be waitin' with the horses. He knows I like to change 'em before I eat—"

In the station house, McCanless was coming back to consciousness. Rolling in the dirt floor, he turned onto his back, his hand rubbing the back of his head, and from outside he could hear the rattle of hoofs and gear.

The coach was coming in.

Jerking upright, he found himself staring into the barrel of a blunt-nosed automatic. Behind it was a thin-faced man.

"Say anything," he assured the stationman in a quiet voice, "and you won't have a head no more."

In back of the house, away from the road, Canfield and Phil Gage heard the coach too.

Easing a glance around the corner, Canfield watched as the coach charged up the road, roaring around the end of the corral and into the yard.

Pressing back behind the wall, Canfield moved his eyes to the far side of the corral. Lying down beneath the fence were Howie Taylor and Rem Sidy.

Canfield thumbed back the hammer on his pistol.

"Get ready," he told Gage.

Swinging around the point of the corral, Jake heard the driver yell to the horses to stop and they came to a rest between the corral and the house.

"Lunch," Jake smiled at Addie, and slipping the handle, he opened the door, stepping out of the coach.

Above him, the driver was standing in the seat.

"Hope this fella can cook," Jake began.

The driver put out a cautioning hand to Jake. "Hold on a minute," he said, his eyes moving over the empty yard. "McCanless—" he called.

"Stand still." A voice from behind the station cut him off.

Jake's muscles tensed.

On the seat, the shotgun messenger's .12 gauge began to ease up.

"Be a foolish thing to do, friend," the voice warned him. "You're covered from the corral too."

Addie Ballard's head came through the door. "What's going on?" she demanded.

"Just sit still," Jake instructed her quietly.

"I will not. I'm—"

"It'd be a good idea," the voice told her, and a man stepped from behind the station. Tall, wearing an old army campaign hat. A huskier, thick-shouldered man followed him.

They were both holding guns.

"Messenger," the taller man said, "throw the scatter-gun down—"

Two more men stood up next to the fence of the corral, leveling guns on the coach.

From inside the station a squat, sandy-haired man stumbled into the open grasping his head. A thin-faced man holding a gun followed him.

Frowning, the messenger put the shotgun down into the boot.

The horses shifted their feet and the coach moaned on its leather braces.

"You all right, Mac?" the driver called to the stationman.

"Sorry," McCanless said. "They come in—"

"That's enough," the man in the campaign hat said, and looked to the men on the seat. "Now the handguns," he ordered them. "Just—"

Out of the corner of his eye Jake caught the movement.

Hopeless and stupid.

The stationman bolted, turning around, slamming his shoulder into the man behind him, rushing him. Stumbling, the thin-faced man shot him, but the weight of the dead man was already carrying them both crashing backward into the pole of the rickety porch, bringing down the roof.

"Mac—" the driver screamed, and at the same time the shotgun messenger dove into the brace of horses, shouting them out.

The horses reared, jerking against the harnesses, then the front two burst out, running.

As the coach jerked beside him, Jake whirled, shoving Addie back inside, grabbing the post between the window and the door, then bounding, managing to get his foot up on the step.

Above him, on the seat of the coach, he heard the driver fire at the two men beside the building, forcing them back around the corner.

The horses charged around the side of the building, the messenger guiding them. The driver fired again, pushing Canfield and Phil Gage down into the dirt. Rolling and coming up, Canfield pumped three quick shots into him, ramming him backward, tumbling him over the roof.

Pushing himself to his feet, Canfield watched the messenger pulling the horses around, swinging through the yard, coming back toward the house, trying to make the road.

Thumbing the hammer of the automatic, he squeezed a shot off at the messenger, but missed. He was moving too fast. Behind him, Rem Sidy and Howie Taylor pounded across the yard.

"You're losin' it," Sidy shouted, raising his new Colt.

"The horses," Canfield warned him, but the old man wasn't listening.

The horses were coming alongside him. Before Canfield could do anything, Rem was swinging a bead on the messenger, pulling the trigger of the automatic frantically, spraying shots into the air.

A slug hit the lead horse in the neck, a second smashed his skull. The animal still ran for a moment, then dead, his legs began folding under him, and he crashed down, twisting into the horse next to him. The rest of the team rammed into him, trying to leap over the dead mound of flesh, tangling themselves in the labyrinth of leather harnesses, and suddenly they were falling too, piling into each other, screaming.

Still hanging on to the side of the coach, Jake barely heard the shots, then saw the horses as they seemed to blend into one another, then felt the tongue of the coach lance into the dirt, ripping into it, snapping, hurling the coach off to one side.

Inside the coach he heard Addie scream, and trying to get to her, he was hurled from the coach, thrown by the momentum, pounding into the rocky dirt, rolling, crashing into the station house wall. And darkness.

For a moment after the coach had tipped, crashing into the ground, Walt Canfield stood stunned, lingering halfway between two motions. The coach was on its side, the wheels revolving slightly, moaning softly, mixing with the cawed breathing of the dazed horses and Canfield's own trembling breath. They all seemed to be pausing, a memory of rage, about to feed on itself. The dead horse, the coach, even the man that had been thrown from the coach and

now slumped against the wall of the station house, seemed
that they would be freed into motion in another second.

Logan came around the side of the building and stopped
flat-footed. "Jesus," he murmured.

His voice seemed to revive the others. Blinking, Rem
Sidy cleared his throat and looked down at the gun. "Nice
piece," he smiled.

Canfield's eyes eased up in an angry sidelong glance at
the old man; then sighing, he shook his head and holstered
his gun.

"Check him," he said to Taylor, and pointed to the man
against the wall, then looked at the coach again. "Let's
take a look," he shrugged, and moved toward the coach
with Gage, Logan, and Sidy following.

As he walked, his eyes were drawn back to the forms of
the horses, and seeing the crushed outline of the messenger,
he stopped.

"Go ahead," he said to Gage, and reaching into his
pocket, he took out his folding knife, turned to the horses,
and began cutting loose those that were still moving.

"Hey," Gage called from the top of the coach, looking
down into it. "I think she's all right," he said, and laughed.
"Yeah, she's all right."

"No thanks to Rem. Get her out," Canfield said, straightening, his hands covered with blood, watching the two he'd
just cut free. Both limped badly. Wiping the blood from
the knife on his pant leg, he slipped it back into his coat
pocket, then drew his gun slowly.

"No use," he said, looking at the two animals, his eyes
softening for a moment; then he raised the gun and shot
them quickly, knocking them back into the dirt.

The gun drifted back down and he put it back into the
leather carefully, his eyes still on the horses, staring now.

"Captain," Taylor said, straightening up from the man
against the wall.

"What?" Canfield's eyes stayed on the horses.

Taylor stumbled toward him. "Captain, this fella's got a goddamn fortune on him. Look at this—"

Dragging his eyes from the horses, Canfield looked around.

Taylor was holding out some money to him. A roll as big as his fist. Reaching out, Canfield took it from him.

"How much you figger is there?" Taylor asked.

"A lot," Canfield answered. "A hellava lot." His eyes went to the man against the wall. "He dead?"

Taylor, more interested in the money, only glanced back at the man. "Yeah, I guess. Looks like it. What about the money?"

"More money for the general. More money for guns."

"Damn," Taylor grinned proudly. "We really done it, didn't we? We really pulled somethin' off."

"Yeah," Canfield nodded, stuffing the money into his shirt pocket. He turned to Phil Gage who was on the ground holding the girl. "Get a horse from the corral and put her on it," he said, then looked to Taylor again. "Burn it," he said.

"What?"

"The house, the coach, the barn," he said. "Burn 'em. I don't want nothin' left standing."

Ten minutes later they were headed up the ridge. Canfield pushed his horse over the top, and seeing Phil Gage on the crest, reined in beside him. The big man was staring back down the slope at what was left of the stage stop. Flames and nightmare shapes.

"Phil—"

"Always hated that," the big man swallowed.

Canfield looked back down at the burning station. "Has to be done. You been in this line of work long enough to know that."

"You'd think so—"

"We got what we came after," he reminded Gage. "And more. We hit it lucky with that money Taylor found. That's gonna set mighty well with the general." He looked at Gage. "Hell, we've had a good day—"

"Yeah," Gage growled, and twisting his horse's head around, ran him up the hill.

Canfield watched him questioningly for a moment, then shrugging, he followed.

# FIVE

He awoke into flames.

Jake swam in dream fires. He thought for a moment that he might be dead or gone to hell, then wrenching up through his own darkness, he saw the flames above him.

He was still against the house wall, and the sky whorled in brightness, white-red and blue.

Falling over onto his stomach, he began crawling, his fingers touching hot char-black pieces of wood that had fallen from the roof. Shoving a passage through them, he grasped the dirt and pulled himself away.

But there was something on fire in front of him too.

The coach.

Turning, he pushed himself toward the corral. Halfway across the yard, he pumped his legs under him, and doubling himself, jacked up into a half-standing position; crawl-running to the corral logs, he fell against them and slumped down.

Sagging in the dirt, his eyes were drawn back to the fire. The flames and the sun seemed to be the same thing, coiling into one another, merging. Even in the corral the heat reddened his skin, and he found himself pushing back through the fence, but the heat from the sun was almost the same. Beneath him, the ground was a blind mirror of the heat, echoing it back toward its source, burning the man's hands.

"Jesus," he choked. "Jesus . . ." His eyes went across the empty corral to the watering trough. Dropping over onto his hands and knees again, he scrambled for the water. Stumbling across the corral, he fell against the trough, ramming his shoulder into the wood. His hands gripped the sides, and hauling himself upward, he slipped across the wood, and felt the water begin to wander over him. Then close around him like a kind of quieter flame.

He lay there for a long time. He could still feel the sun and hear the flames and smell the dying wood, but they were a dream away, in another place, and he didn't move.

Drifting, he knew why water was such a good death.

The thought of dying filled him with a gentleness like laughter, and he wondered about just easing into the water and being rid of the heat and pain once and for all.

And suddenly it made him angry.

His hands folded down on the wood, lifting him up.

He wasn't going to die.

The water drifted back and away and he was out of it, standing. Falling over the edge into the boiling dirt. Alive again.

His eyes moved sluggishly over the station. All the buildings were on fire.

"Bastards," he whispered thickly, and pushing himself up against the watering trough, he wrestled himself out of his coat, dipped it into the water, and dragged it back over his head, making a shelter.

He drifted again, slept again, and awoke again.

Lifting the coat away slowly, he squinted in the afternoon sunlight. The buildings were gone. Only warped leavings remained. Black, still blurred with smoke.

Grasping the side of the trough, Jake pulled himself up. He scooped up the tepid water with his hands and drank two long drinks, then made himself stop. Standing, he walked back across the corral toward what was left of the station. He leaned against the log fence and looked himself over.

His shoulder and head throbbed. He put his hand up and there was a crusting of blood down the side of his face. His shirt had been torn open and his shoulder had been cut, but not badly. Running his hands over his trunk and legs, he could find nothing else.

He smiled weakly. "Landin' on my head musta saved me," he mused, and tugging his eyes up, he looked over what was left of the stage station.

It seemed like nothing had ever existed there except ruin.

Under the smoking rubble of the porch, he could make out a man's legs. The stationman's. Whatever his name was.

His eyes moved to the skeleton of the coach and the bodies of the horses and the man blended among them.

Jake didn't know his name either and that bothered him. He wished he knew their names at least. Now they were nameless as well as faceless and dead.

Anonymous. Blended with the dust. Mingled with flame.

Swallowing, Jake shook his head. There was no time for that. They were dead and he was alive and he had to find a way to keep living.

He looked back to the water. At least there was that. He could wait until tomorrow when the next stage came through. If one ran tomorrow.

He leaned back against the fence. It didn't matter. He had water. A stage would come and he would get into town, then go on to—

His hand jumped to his coat pocket, working in reflex before his memory did.

The money. His hand tore through the pocket.

It was gone.

Wheeling, he ran back to the watering trough, plunging his hands into the water; finding nothing, he dropped to his knees, looking around in the dirt.

Standing again, he stumbled back across the corral to the adobe wall of the house. There were smoking boards where he had been lying. Using his boot, he kicked them around, his eyes combing the wood and dirt.

Under his boot, something gleamed dully in the dirt.

Leaning down, he brushed the dust away and picked it up.

It was his knife.

Gripping it tightly by the handle, he wandered back into the open. He found tracks and followed them to the road. They went across it, then southeast toward the mountains.

They had it, he nodded.

He knew they had it.

Easing down into a squatting position, he forced a calm through himself, trying to sort things out.

There would most likely be another stage through tomorrow. But that wouldn't do any good. He would have to go on into the railhead to get a horse. That meant another day and a half, and another half day back. Two days.

He shook his head. It was too long. Their tracks would be gone by then.

Standing, he looked off toward the mountains.

There was only one way of doing it. He had to go after them.

Now.

# SIX

Riding, feeling movement under her, Addie Ballard began to gather the edges of coherence back again.

She had been in the coach, then running, tipping, crashing, then nothing. She had awakened in the saddle; the rhythm of the horse lulled her awake.

She tried to move and found her hands were immobile, and looking down she saw they were tied. Her eyes came up suddenly, widening.

Two men were riding on either side of her. One narrow-faced, sallow. The other thick-shouldered.

The thick-shouldered man smiled.

"What're you doin?" she asked, and was amazed at the sound of her voice. Ragged. Old.

"Nothin', miss," the man answered. "You just stay quiet a while longer."

Looking down at the ropes around her wrists, she wrenched against them, trying to get free. "Why am I tied?" she demanded, struggling with her whole body now. "What are you doing?" she screamed. "What are you doing?"

The thick-shouldered man halted his horse, then reaching out, grasping her shoulder, tried to calm her.

"Now, miss, you—"

In front of them, another man turned his horse and rode back to them. She blinked, looking at him. She had seen him someplace before. He was tall, wearing an old campaign hat.

"Miss Ballard," the man in the campaign hat said, in a level businesslike tone. "Be quiet or I'll knock you quiet."

Addie blinked, her heart hammering in her chest, and she forced herself to calm down. No one had ever talked to her like that before. And she knew by his eyes that he meant it.

"Who are you?" she asked. "Why am I tied?"

"Miss Ballard," the man frowned. "We ain't got the time." He looked to the thick-shouldered man.

"Gage, she yells again, hit her."

The man named Gage stiffened. "I ain't taken to sluggin' women yet."

The tall man glared at him. "Maybe it's time you started," he said, and pulled his horse around, heading out again.

The thick-shouldered man's eyes shadowed slightly, a flicker of regret in them, and he looked at Addie. He tried to smile, but only his lips found the pose.

"I'd do as he says," he instructed her, and spurred his horse out.

Jake sat down on the edge of the water trough, exhausted.

He had spent an hour roaming through the ruins and found nothing.

"Damn," he whispered, and dipping his hand into the trough, he sipped some water. Then his eyes wandering over the station, he did some accounting.

He had no horse. No way to carry water. And no food.

He pushed his coat back and lifted his knife from its leather.

That was it.

One damned old Green River.

He smiled ruefully. Well, it was something and there was that to be thankful for.

He lifted his eyes toward the mountains. They were a day, or a day and a half away. Probably three on foot.

There would be food and water up there.

His eyes came back to the desert. There was food and water there too. Just a little tricky getting to it.

"Damn," he grumbled.

He should be sensible and wait for the stage. Let it go. He could make more money.

He shook his head. That meant time. And he was fifty-five years old.

No telling how long it would take him to make three thousand again. He had two lucky winters in the last four years. His luck might not be that good again.

His eyes went to the mountains.

No, if he was going to Australia and get some land, it had to be now. In five years a lot of that land would be gone. Gone to fence builders.

Standing, Jake slipped the knife back in its sheath, and leaned over the trough. He drank his fill; then, taking off his coat, he soaked it with water, and did the same with his new shirt.

He tugged the coat back on and draped his shirt over his head.

Then started walking.

# SEVEN

Addie Ballard rode quietly as the man she'd heard one of the others call Canfield led his men through the dry twisted country of rock, sandstone, and small stunted juniper. The sun burned her face and hands, and her thick blond hair matted in sweat on the back of her neck and fell curving in her eyes. She had lost her new hat.

They rode for a long time. Through the ragged boulders, and up onto a high sandstone ridge. The horses' hoofs rattled over the stone, echoing back on her, filling the air.

"Water pocket," she heard the leader say, and her eyes came up.

The horses wound down a small slope of rock toward a bright circle of water.

"Water and rest 'em," the leader said, and they reined in. The one called Gage dismounted and lifted Addie down out of the saddle. The men knelt beside the horses as they pushed their snouts into the liquid.

Addie watched as the animals put their hoofs into the pool, and the men scooped at the water, spitting some back then taking more.

Canfield stood up from the sump, wiping his mouth; taking out his folding knife, he walked to Addie and cut her free, then gestured toward the water.

"Best have some," he said to her. "It's a ways yet to the next."

Looking at the now murky pool, Addie shook her head. "It's dirty," she protested. "The animals—"

The leader frowned. "I told you to drink, Miss Ballard," he said in a controlled voice. "Now do it—"

Addie stepped away from him. "I'm not an animal," she snapped. "You sonofabitch—"

Canfield stepped into her, grasping her arms. Fighting against him, she jerked one hand free, raking it across his face.

He stopped suddenly, staring at her, his hands trembling.

Then he moved. Quickly. Violently. Without warning.

His hand darted up, wrapping her twice in the chin, sending her stumbling back. Catching her, Canfield hit her again with one hand, the other grasping the collar of her dress, tearing it open, wrenching the buttons off. Turning her around, he ripped the loose material down the front, beginning to expose her breasts—

Then somebody else was there.

The big man, Gage, was stepping between them, shoving Canfield back.

Canfield whirled on him, drawing his gun, leveling it at Gage's stomach, the hammer hanging poised.

Swallowing, Canfield straightened, the anger paling his face.

"Don't ever do that again," he whispered to the thick-shouldered man.

"I don't make war on women," Gage growled.

"They're like anybody else," Canfield said, and bringing the pistol down, lowered the hammer slowly, holstered it, looking at Addie.

"From now on," he breathed, "when I say to do somethin', you do it. You got that?"

Trembling, covering herself, Addie nodded her response.

Canfield nodded. "Get her on a horse," he said.

Gage turned to her, and taking her arm, started for the horses. Walking, she could feel the men's eyes following her.

"Walt—" the thin-faced one began.

The leader looked at him, and realizing what he wanted, shook his head wearily. "Jesus, Jed," he sighed. "Keep your mind on business."

"Been a long time," the old man put in.

Canfield went to his horse and mounted. "Be a while longer," he said.

Gage helped Addie into the saddle.

"Phil," Canfield said.

Gage hesitated beside her, looking up.

"I'm in charge here. You ever get between me and what I've got to do again, I'll kill you. Friend or not."

Gage stared at him. "You can try," he said.

A tight smile touched Canfield's mouth, and nodding, he turned his horse out.

Gage watched for a moment, then taking Addie's reins, he pulled himself into the saddle.

Addie looked at him. "Thank you," she said.

Gage glanced at her. "Yeah," he said, and spurred his horse out.

Jake Hooker set a good steady pace for himself. The horse tracks leading from the stage station were plain, but he knew they would be gone before long, taken by the hot wind that rushed over the naked rock and through the dust.

The late afternoon sun pushed down hard on the man as he weaved through the rocks and greasewood, juniper and prickly pear. His feet ached in the new boots, and the muscles in his legs were numb. It had been a long time since he'd done any traveling by foot. He had never been fond of it.

After walking for nearly three hours, he stopped, and peeling off the coat, he squeezed water from it. Behind him, the sun knitted into the labyrinth of mesas, ridges, and hills, the yellow-red light metamorphosing them, making its color theirs, molding them with shadow and songs of night.

Jake wiped his mouth, and rubbed the water over his face, then looked forward, his eyes moving over the ground.

He was going to lose his light before long, then he would have nothing but a guess to lead him.

His eyes went to the tracks again, looking backward and forward.

They had been heading southeast, steady. Toward the edge of the Dos Lobos where they came up from the hills at Miller's Store.

Jake considered it a moment. If they were headed for Mexico that would be the quickest way. Around the foot of the mountains and down. Stop at Miller's for supplies, then head on. And there weren't any towns this way. Just Miller's.

Jake nodded. It was a gamble, but by walking all night, heading toward Miller's, he could close a lot of ground between him and the raiders. They would have to stop in another thirty minutes or so, and he could gain a lot of time on them.

"Some days," he grumbled wearily. Moving was the only choice he had.

Shaking his head, he started out again.

# EIGHT

Night gathered around Addie, muting away the mesas, following them as she and the men descended into a canyon. Steep walls rose up around them, bringing more darkness, and suddenly it was night. For a moment, Addie thought they were going into a cave, but looking up, beyond the walls of the canyon she could see the sky and the faint scrawl of sunlight dying.

Her eyes came back down, resting on the man in the lead, her stomach twisting, nearly cramping with fear.

They wouldn't hurt her, she kept telling herself. They wouldn't. And perhaps someone would help her. She swallowed. Nightmares happened to other people. To people who were only names in the newspapers. Like characters in a book. Not real.

After a while, the canyon widened, and they skirted several small hills, and Addie thought she could hear the wind blowing through leaves. Squinting into the darkness, she saw the blossoming shapes of trees. Cottonwoods and salt cedar. Riding across a paddock of grass, they came to a stream, crossed it, and the men began dismounting beneath the trees.

Gage stepped to the ground, held his hand out for Addie, and helped her down. Turning to his horse, he unstrung his canteen and handed it to her.

"Get some fresh," he said. "Wash your face, you might feel some better."

Addie took the canteen numbly and nodded, turning back down the slight incline to the stream.

Emptying the canteen, she pushed it beneath the water. Her eyes came up slowly, looking back over the ground from where they'd come. Folding into twilight now. Rock and sandstone, misshapen bushes and trees. Crossing the stream, she could be hidden almost immediately by an outcropping of boulders and those small bushes, she—

"Go ahead," a voice said behind her.

Her eyes jerked around. Canfield was just up the hill watching her.

"Go ahead," he repeated.

Snatching the canteen from the water, she stood shaking her head. "I wasn't—"

"Sure you were," he nodded, then pointed off down the canyon. "But a woman like you'd be dead inside a day out there alone. Least going with us you'll be alive. And bein' alive's a lot better'n bein' dead."

Trembling she felt tears struggling in her. "Please," she whispered. "What do you want? Please tell me why you've taken me."

Walt Canfield stared at her for a moment, then shrugged. "No reason not to now, I guess. You're a hostage, ma'am."

"A . . ."

"Hostage," Canfield repeated. "You heard of the revolution in Mexico?"

"Yes," she nodded. "But I still don't understand. What have I got to do with that?"

"Nothing," Canfield answered. "Except that your father has a hellava lot of money and we need some of it fast." Canfield reached into his pocket and withdrew a cigar, placing it in his mouth. "A man named Hoffer has some Vickers machine guns, rifles, and more of these—" He withdrew the gun at his side. "This is a Colt .45 automatic. Single link, which means they don't jam as easy as the old double link." He frowned, seeing Addie didn't understand the workings of pistols, and placed it back in his holster. "Let's just say they're a damn good gun. Anyway, Hoffer wants ten thousand for the whole bunch. Used to"—Canfield paused, striking a match—"we'd just come up and rob a bank." He puffed on the cigar. "But there are a couple of things wrong with that method right now." He waved the match out. "First, we've robbed an awful lot of banks lately in New Mexico and Texas and they're layin' for us, and second, there might not be ten thousand in one bank, which means we'd have to rob two—or a big one, which pushes up the risk factor considerably. And that's bad tactics." He drew on the cigar slowly. "Your daddy is well known in southwestern New Mexico. And his reputation's been growin' in Mexico because he's been buyin' a lot of cattle down there. Makin' a lot of profit because of the war. The general figured it was time he reciprocated. Easiest way of doin' it's through you."

Addie listened, unbelieving. It was like hearing somebody talk about business. The same calculation that monotoned her father's voice. Buying and selling. Commodities.

She shook her head. "It will never work . . ."

Canfield's eyes narrowed. "Sure it will," he assured her. "Nothin's gonna stop it. It's already set in motion."

"How?"

Canfield frowned. "Don't matter. Less you know about that part of it the better. One thing—the less trouble you cause, the better off you and your daddy are gonna be. You got that?"

Addie swallowed. "Yes," she whispered.

"Right," Canfield nodded, motioning her back up the hill. "Now let's get started on some food."

Jake came up the sandstone ridge and across it to the small pool of water. Kneeling down beside it, he drank slowly, then, standing up, shivered.

The night had brought a chill and the wetness from his coat still lingered in his shirt, biting into his skin.

He was starting around the small pool when he saw the

marks of hoofs in the sandstone. Kneeling again, he touched them and looked off to the southeast.

They had come this way.

Nodding, pushing himself upright, he walked out again.

# NINE

All through dinner, Addie could feel the men's eyes on her. Especially the grizzle-bearded old man and the thin-faced one.

Following each movement. Examining her.

She pushed more beans into her mouth and tried not to think of them, or the present. Something would happen. It had to. Someone would help her and she would get back to school. Back to where it was safe.

She chewed the pasty beans. Nightmares happened to other people, she kept telling herself.

Other people.

After the meal, Canfield told her to do the dishes. She gathered up the plates, and with Gage following, she carried them down to the stream.

Dipping the plates in the stream, she scrubbed at them with her fingers as Gage sat down behind her on a rock.

"Do a little more good," he suggested, "if you use some of the stream gravel."

Nodding, she tried it. Scooping sand into the tin. As she worked her eyes slipped back up to the big man.

"Will he kill me?" she finally asked.

Gage's eyes darkened. "Likely not," he answered, after a moment's consideration. "Wouldn't serve any purpose—and Walt's a purposeful man. Does everything by the book."

"By the book?"

"Old army expression. Means everything is calculated to an end."

"You were in the Army together?"

"We were both in the cavalry, but we knew each other after."

Addie scrubbed the plates. "You . . . don't seem like him."

Gage's face lined slightly. "Used to be a lot more. But people change. Some a bit more than others."

Addie put down the plate she was working on, swallowing, glancing up toward the camp, then back at the thick-shouldered man, trying to build her courage.

"Can you help me, Mr. Gage? My father will pay you—"

Gage was already frowning, shaking his head. "There's some things more important than money. I don't like bringing you into this, but there's no other way. Now finish up and let's get back."

Up the slope, Canfield settled on his blankets with a cup of coffee.

Across the fire, Sidy sat hunkered, glancing down at the girl and Gage at each sound of the water splashing. On his blankets, Logan was watching her too, his eyes holding her quietly.

Sidy's eyes bobbed up nervously as Taylor ambled in from the horses and knelt down beside the fire.

"They're secure," he reported to Canfield, and poured himself a cup of coffee.

Canfield nodded.

Taylor sat for a moment, then smiled. "Hellava day, wasn't it," he said.

Sidy glanced at him. "Huh?"

"Hellava day," Taylor said again, and cocked his head. "This is some life. Excitement and all."

"Yeah," Sidy nodded absently. "Quite a life."

Taylor mused again, sipping his coffee. "Know what I'm gonna do when this war's over—"

Sidy's attention was still on the girl.

"—gonna get me one of them hand-tool, silver saddles," Taylor went on, "and ride right back up to my pa's farm

and show him. Always said I'd never amount to nothin'."
He looked to Sidy, who wasn't really listening. "How 'bout
you, Rem?" he probed.

The old man's eyes came around. "Huh? Oh—I don't
know. Buy me a place down near Brownsville, I reckon.
Sun shines all year round. Get me a big old easy chair
and sit on the front porch and bake this leg." He rubbed
his thigh.

"Yeah," Taylor nodded slowly. "You know—" he began,
then saw that Rem wasn't listening. He set his cup down.
"Well, best hit the blankets," he said.

Rem mumbled something, and shrugging, Taylor got up
and went to his bedroll.

At the fire, Sidy stood up suddenly, rubbing his thigh.

"Sure could use a drink," he sighed, frustration tightening his voice.

"Have some coffee," Canfield said.

"Keeps me awake," Sidy said. "'Sides, I think it's painin'
my leg."

Canfield's cup paused on the way to his mouth. "What?"

"My leg." Sidy massaged his thigh. "All stiff'n sore like.
Coffee done it. Poison in it."

"Poison?"

Sidy nodded. "A mite. That's what gives you the thumps.
And's makin' my leg ache."

"Why do you keep drinkin' it?"

Sidy shrugged. "I like it."

Canfield eased back into his saddle. "Jesus," he sighed.

Sidy glanced at the girl as she and Gage started back
up the slope.

"You know, Walt, I'd sure like to—"

"No," Canfield cut him off immediately.

Sidy looked at him. "How'd you know what I was gonna
ask?"

"Wasn't hard. And the answer's still no."

"Why not, Walt? Hell, for the whole bunch of us, it

wouldn't take too long." He grinned. "Now you can't tell me you wouldn't like a little—"

"I'm tellin' you, Rem." Canfield's voice hardened. "Business first. You can have all the women you want when we get done with this."

Addie came up the slope, passing by the old man, putting the plates and frying pan down by the fire. Then she went to the blankets that had been put down for her. Gage sat down on his roll and leaned back against his saddle.

Sidy's eyes followed the girl; then shaking his head in frustration, he went to his own blankets complaining under his breath.

"Damn," Canfield sighed, tossing the last of his coffee away. "Let's get some sleep," he said, "we got work to do." Putting the cup down, he pulled his hat over his eyes and eased back.

Across the fire Sidy's eyes were still on the girl.

And Logan's.

Addie turned in her blankets for almost an hour trying to sleep, but couldn't. The ground was too hard, and the breathing of the men seemed to press in on her.

Sitting up, she pushed the blanket aside, and looked over the men. They were asleep. At least they were all quiet.

She lifted her eyes to the darkness beyond the firelight, then closed them quietly. She could get up and walk away. But Canfield was right. She would be dead in one day out there.

She would wait. Her father would pay the money and she would be safe. Her stomach trembled. Him and his damned money.

Opening her eyes again, she shivered and clasped her hands to her shoulders. She started to lay down again, then realized the cold had stimulated her kidneys.

Frowning, she stood up, and walked out of camp down the hill angling along the stream into the brush.

She had found a clear spot when she heard the rustling of leaves behind her.

Startled, she jerked up, turning around.

The narrow-faced one, Logan, was smiling at her. "Go on," he nodded. The smile widened.

She straightened, fear twisting in her throat.

"I was just—"

"I know," he nodded. "Don't pay me no mind."

"Please," she swallowed. "I'll be back in a minute."

Logan stepped toward her. "You're a shy one, ain't you?"

Addie trembled. She tried to step back, but her legs seemed leaden. Numb.

Logan closed the space between them. So close to her now she could smell his breath and sweat. His hand came up. Touching her breast.

"No," she murmured, her voice dry, more a moan than anything else.

"You ain't the prettiest thing in the world," he whispered. "But you'll do—"

His hand tightened on her breast, and she tried to move back again.

"Stand still," he snapped. "Just—"

He pulled her to him then, his hands clasping her arms. Tight. Pushing her down.

"No," she whispered. "No—"

"Come on," he half whined, half growled, shoving her harder, but Addie twisted, tearing her arm loose, jerking away from him.

"Goddammit," he barked, and she saw his free hand cocking back. Gathering into a fist.

Trying to get out of the way, she reeled blindly, slamming into him. The contact panicked her, and bolting, she began to kick and slap, flailing wildly to get loose again.

And fighting, her knee found a sudden softness between his legs.

Logan's wind exploded from him, and gagging, he stumbled back, the hand gripping her arm weakening.

Wrenching her arm, she tore away, the momentum carrying her backward, stumbling into the brush.

Logan's hands sank to his middle, and he tried to scream, but there was no sound, only a rasping wet caw in his throat.

His eyes fixed on her a mixture of pain and hate and he staggered forward reaching for her.

Turning, she crawled, her feet scraping, propelling her away.

Above her, she could hear Logan crashing toward her, and looking up, she saw him slump to his knees, his hands still stretched toward her, the hatred in his eyes stronger than the pain now.

"Kill you," his voice bubbled. "Kill . . ." And he lunged forward diving for her, his hand catching her foot weakly.

Frantically, she reeled, jerking against his hold. His other hand came forward, reaching to secure his grasp. With her free foot, she kicked at his hand, slamming her shoe heel into it again and again, hammering bone and flesh.

His hold weakened, then gave, and still kicking, she pulled away from him; getting over onto her hands and knees, she staggered to her feet, and ran, charging into the stream.

The coldness of the water startled her. Behind her, she could hear Logan on the ground, his breath aching through him, crying.

She clamored through the water, onto the bank, stumbling over the pebbles and rocks, running again.

On the other bank, Logan had pushed to his knees, his breath coming back to him.

"Canfield," he cry-moaned, then stronger. "Canfield—"

The voice jerked through her, bursting like another kind of energy, sending her rushing between the hills and up the canyon.

# TEN

Canfield bolted upright in his blankets; then hearing the cry again, he tossed the cover aside and was on his feet, running, slamming through the brush, drawing his Colt.

Charging down along the creek, he saw Logan on the ground, holding his crotch, and his first impulse was to laugh.

Then he realized.

"The girl," he yelled back up the hill, and Gage came down beside him.

"She's not in camp," the big man said.

Turning, Canfield's eyes swept the creek, back down the canyon.

Nothing.

He looked back to Logan and rushed to him. Leaning down, he grasped Logan's shirt, pulling him up. His skinny face was white, trembling his pain.

"Where is she, Jed?"

Logan's hand pushed out toward the creek and he managed to choke something, but Canfield couldn't understand it.

Standing, Canfield walked to the creek's edge and stared into the darkness.

"Miss Ballard," he called, forcing calm into his voice. "You might as well come on back. You ain't got a chance out there."

He waited. Silence.

"Miss Ballard," he called again, the anger edging into his voice. "Goddammit, don't be stupid—" His hands squeezed shut. "All right," he nodded, "but you're not gonna like it when we find you."

He looked back at his men. Sidy and Taylor had come down now too.

"Just went to sleep," complained Sidy.

"Find her," Canfield snapped, then motioned to Gage. "Help me get him back up, then we'll look too."

Addie huddled down behind a rock. The sound of Canfield's voice had come like a shot, and she had gotten down behind the first thing she could find. It was nearly a minute before she could breathe again.

Then he stopped yelling, and that frightened her even more.

Her eyes jerked up into the darkness of strange forms and it suddenly seemed like water washing around her, reaching, trying quietly to take her. Pushing herself further back into the rocks, she could hear the rustle of voices from the direction of the creek.

She could feel the tears coming, and fighting, she shook her head.

No.

They would be after her in a minute, and she couldn't start crying. They would hear her.

Turning, she forced herself away from the rocks back into the main part of the canyon. She slipped to a rock and looked back toward the creek.

A vague fluttering of the firelight nudged the darkness from behind the two small hills.

The mixing sound of boots on rocks and voices tugged her eyes up like an animal's. Turning again, panic exploded through her, thickening the air in her lungs. Running, she fell, stumbling across sharp rocks, scraping her legs. Clamoring to her feet again, she weaved a few more steps and fell again.

Tears wet her face and she could taste their salt in her mouth. Trembling, she squeezed the sobs back in her

Athens Regional Library
Athens, Georgia

188462

throat. She looked back toward the creek. A form moved between the hills. Coming toward her.

Lifting herself up, she ran again, plunging deeper into the walls of the canyon, feeling them rise up around her, drawing toward her.

Running, she collided with a large rock, and stumbling, fell off to one side, slipping down beside it, her breath raking through her, pulsing in her chest like somebody hitting her. Hesitating, she looked back, then turning to get up, she noticed a space below the boulder beside her. Easing down, she could make out a small opening where the rock had balanced, then a greater space where the lower rock fell away.

Behind her, she heard the scrape of boots.

Her breath rattled through her, and looking back to the opening, she swallowed. There might be something down there.

The sound of boots came closer.

She squeezed her eyes shut and opened them again. She remembered Logan's eyes. And Canfield's warning that afternoon. She couldn't go back.

Lowering herself to her stomach, she pressed herself between the rocks. The smell of dirt filled her nose, and pushing forward, she suddenly jerked back. Something moved.

Up the canyon the footfalls were louder.

Forcing herself on down she wriggled the rest of the way beneath the boulder and pulled her feet in after her hugging them up against her chest, then lying quietly.

In the darkness, further down the crack something rustled. Small. Crawling.

Her heart felt like it was ripping through her chest.

The footfalls were near her now.

Sweat and tears burned in her eyes and the cuts on her face.

Down the crack it moved again.

She choked back a moan in her throat.

The boots were nearly beside her. Snapping small bits of

gravel. Through the brush. Coming alongside her. Stopping beside her foot.

Deeper in the crack the rustling whispered toward her. For a moment, she thought she was going to scream or vomit, then the rustling moved on and out the crack away from the rock.

"See anything?" A voice pulled her eyes back around. She couldn't see anything, but could hear somebody else joining the man beside her.

"See anything?" the voice asked again.

"No." It was Sidy; she recognized the wheeze in his voice.

"Jesus, old Walt's riled."

"Yeah. Hell, there ain't nothin' out here. So goddamn dark you could spit on a moose and not see'm."

Silence. A shuffling of boots.

"Crap," Sidy wheezed, "let's go on back. I'm tired of this."

Addie lay still as they walked away, and stayed where she was for another hour. Crying without sound.

Then pushing her feet back out, she crawled from her hiding place and stood up, looking out into the darkness.

She was free.

And that frightened her almost as much as the alternative.

When Canfield climbed back up the slope into camp, the others were already there. Ambling to the fire, he knelt down and poured himself a cup of coffee.

"How's your jewels?" he asked Logan.

Logan shrugged grudgingly, embarrassed. "All right, I reckon."

Canfield tasted his coffee.

"What were you doin' down there, Jed?" he asked slowly.

Logan shook his head. "Saw her leave camp. Thought I oughta keep an eye on her."

Nodding, Canfield's eyes swept the others.

"Nothin', huh?"

No answers.

"Yeah." The leader frowned resolutely.

Taylor cleared his throat. "Awful dark in that canyon, Walt. Maybe tomorrow."

"No," he answered, standing up. "We ain't got the time."

Taylor blinked and looked at Sidy, then back again. "You're lettin' her go?"

"You hard of hearin', boy? That's exactly what I said."

Taylor stared up at him. "But the money, Walt. Without the girl—"

"I covered that," Canfield answered. "In this kind of an operation you always have an edge—"

Taylor shook his head. "I don't—"

"The money," Canfield explained; "it's already on its way."

"Hold on." Logan sat upright. "You mean you ain't goin' after that bitch come mornin'?"

"No need to. We can get the money without her."

"She kicked me," Logan protested.

"You'll mend."

Logan swallowed, the veins on his neck cording with anger. "No goddam woman's gonna kick me in the groin and get away with it."

"She has," Canfield answered.

Logan stared at him a moment, then nodding, knowing it was no use to argue, turned stiffly to his blankets.

Canfield looked at the others. "Get some sleep," he told them. "We got work to do."

Sidy sat down on his bedroll and looked up at Canfield.

"Hey, Walt—"

"Yeah."

"How come you brought her along? Why not just have some fun with her and shoot her?"

"Because her daddy would have handed the money over a lot easier if we had her."

"Yeah." Sidy blinked. "I guess he would have at that. Huh." He cocked his head, still thinking about it as he lay back on his blankets. "Huh . . ."

Across the fire, Phil Gage knelt down and poured himself

the dregs of the coffee. Even before he spoke, Canfield could see the weight of his thoughts in his face.

The big man's eyes came up slowly.

"You're goin' to kill him, ain't you?" he asked Canfield.

"If he puts up a fight, I—"

"I know you, Walt," Gage interrupted, "and you'll kill him outright before he has a chance to put up any kind of fight."

Canfield's eyes hardened. "Yeah," he nodded, "I will. It's the best way of doin' it. You know that." His eyes narrowed. "What the hell is it with you lately anyhow, Phil? First the girl, now her old man. You act like you're gettin' religion."

"No." Gage shook his head. "Not quite."

"What then? Somethin's sure as hell off center with you."

Gage shrugged his big shoulders. "It's . . . a little hard to explain, just out like that."

Canfield's mouth tightened. "I want to know," he pressed the big man. "I got to know if I can depend on you."

"You have before."

"Yeah," Canfield acknowledged. "I have. But I got a lot ridin' this time—"

"So have a lot of others—" Gage cut in.

Canfield looked up. "Who?"

"The ones we're fightin' this for. The people of Mexico."

Canfield stared back at the big man, then began to smile as if it were a joke.

"Jesus, Phil," he grinned. "You're soundin' like a god-damned patriot."

"I believe in this war, if that's what you mean."

"Damn—" Canfield grinned, then laughed. "Damned if I don't think you're serious. You've turned patriot on me, Phil. Gone soft in the head."

The muscles in Gage's chest and shoulders tensed beneath his shirt, and a flicker of anger narrowed his eyes. "Maybe to your way of thinkin', Walt."

Canfield shook his head. "What done it? A woman? That's usually it."

Gage frowned. "No," he answered. "That time I got shot

up down in the Sierras. The people that took care of me. They were good people. I'd've died without 'em." His mouth tightened. "Soldiers shot'em down for helpin' me. No warnin'. No nothin'. Just rode up and shot'em." He swallowed. "Now I'm about to do the same thing."

Canfield sighed, shaking his head. "Sounds like you got morals along with your patriotism. It won't work. You can't have it both ways."

"Both ways?"

"Your morals, Phil. What about kidnapin'. Don't they include kidnapin'?"

Gage's eyes fell. "That's different—I—"

"Bullshit," Canfield growled. "You made an allowance. You're gonna have to make another. It all comes down to winnin'. Nothin' more. The rest are just excuses. If it's between Ballard and the war, what's your choice gonna be?"

Gage's face was dark. "You know the answer to that," he said.

Canfield nodded. "Then let's get some sleep," he said.

Frowning, Gage stood up. "Yeah," he agreed.

Canfield looked at him. "Phil—"

Gage hesitated.

"You're a good soldier. Don't let sentiment get in your way. It'll get you killed. By the book is the only way to get anything done."

Gage stared at him; then nodding, he silently tossed away the dregs of the coffee and went to his blankets.

He lay on them for a long time, staring up into the darkness.

It had all gotten twisted somehow. Nothing was clear any more.

His eyes moved across the creek. Even the girl's escape. In a way he was glad. But that was twisted too. It would be the thing that killed her father.

They would both have a hand in it.

He and the girl.

# ELEVEN

Addie ran for a long time, and when she couldn't run any more she walked. Night and rocks and unknown sounds blended around her, pushing her on, and finally she couldn't walk any more. Slumping down beside a rock, she told herself she would rest for a minute, just a minute.

And was instantly asleep.

Consciousness came back to her with the beginnings of the morning light. Touching her with the gentleness of a hesitant companion.

She retreated into sleep again for a moment, then bolted upright, pushing herself to her feet, her eyes searching the gray light, and turning, she was moving again, running again.

Jed Logan rustled out of his blankets, and sitting up, looked to the canyon rim. It would be light soon.

Standing, he glanced at the others. Still asleep. Nodding, he lifted his eyes to the creek and touched his crotch.

"Damn," he whispered, and reached down hefting up his saddle.

Turning down the hill toward the horses, his gaze lingered on Canfield for a moment, then he went on.

Canfield or no Canfield, he thought, no woman was going to kick him in the groin and get away with it.

Jake Hooker came down a small folding of hills into an arroyo. Crossing it, he angled toward a morning-dark mesa.

He was tired now. A gnawing weariness bled through him,

tugging at him like a half-remembered chant, but he ignored it, and kept moving his feet.

Coming into a patch of peppergrass, Jake knelt down. White flowers shifted in the breeze, and leaning to the cleft leaves, he licked the moisture from them. There wasn't much water there and what was there was sharp, nearly bitter, with the tang of the leaves, but he got enough to dampen his palate.

Standing again, he shouldered the coat and moved forward.

He wished for a good pair of antelope moccasins lined with buffalo grass for softness, coolness, and warmth. Going barefoot would have been almost as good as these goddamn store-boughts.

It took him an hour to get by the mesa, and when he did, rustlings of morning light began to probe through the joshua and sandstone. Not light yet, but the dream of it.

He came around giant naked pillars of rock in front of the mesa, along another ridge line, and descended toward a canyon.

The ground dropped away, suddenly scooping into the rock, making a deep wide channel scattered with boulders.

Jake was starting down when he saw the flicker of movement deep in the cut.

Faint and quick.

Without thinking, he was dropped, crouching against the wall of the canyon, slipping his knife from its scabbard.

Waiting.

The wind carried the drift of a lark's pierce. And quiet again.

Then the rattle of gravel. Light footfalls, then scraping.

Coming quick, Jake pushed the knife forward, cutting edge up.

Gravel snapped against itself.

Lifting himself, Jake slipped down through a stand of boulders, skinning along a narrow crack between the great rocks, then crawled up one of the great humps, easing up into the open, bringing the knife up to his side, ready.

He eased over the boulder, and starting down it, he saw the figure below him, partially hidden by the curve of the stone. Stepping outward, and jumping, he brought the knife down on the figure, ready to plunge it into him.

In the air, he realized the figure was not a man but a girl, and pulling the knife up, he managed to miss her as he hit the ground.

In front of him, the girl reeled, startled by the noise, and screamed.

Closing on her quickly, he slammed his hand into her mouth, knocking her backward, off her feet, both of them slamming into the hard dirt.

The girl struggled beneath him, biting his hand, punching her knee into his stomach, her hands like claws raking at his face. Jerking his hand from her mouth, she screamed again, in a mixture of panic and rage.

"Miss—" he said, but she screamed again, raking her hands across his face.

Jake tried to get her hands down and his hand back over her mouth, but she kept struggling. Bringing his free hand up, he hit her in the jaw, knocking her back. She slumped to the ground, unconscious and finally quiet.

Jed Logan heard something.

He had just turned his horse along a column of rock when he heard it.

Muffled, then clear. A scream, maybe. Then nothing. But he was sure he'd heard it.

Pulling his horse in, he waited, hoping to hear it again. He'd been riding back and forth an hour or more now, slowly making toward the head of the canyon. He waited nearly a full minute, but there was nothing more.

"Damn," he muttered, frowning, and glancing back down the canyon, then up at the sky, he noted it was coming on morning. The others would be rousing in a bit, and he needed to get back before Canfield knew he was gone. Bringing the girl back would help some.

And besides. She'd kicked him.

His eyes moved back up the canyon. That sound was the first sign he'd had, and he wasn't giving it up now.

His hand touched his crotch.

Not now, he thought, and spurred his animal out.

It took a minute for Jake to recognize the girl. She had been the one on the coach yesterday. Addie Ballard.

"What the hell are you doin' out here?" he whispered. Touching her face, he brushed away the dirt and examined where he'd hit her in the jaw, and winced slightly. It was going to swell.

"You're in fine shape, hoss," he frowned. "Taken to hittin' on females."

He looked at her jaw again, then moved his eyes down. Her dress was torn, and part of her breast exposed.

Tugging the material over, he covered her and finished looking her over. The bottom of her dress was torn too.

"Looks like you been havin' a hard time of it," he whispered, then touched her face.

"Miss—" he said. "Miss—"

Addie moaned softly, her hands fluttering, then jerked up suddenly, the pain in her jaw making her head whirl. Her glazed eyes moved to Jake.

"Now you're all right, miss," he said. "You're just fine."

She backed away from him, her eyes widening.

"You know me," he smiled. "Remember from the coach? Jake Hooker."

Recognition flickered in her gaze. "You hit me."

"Well"—Jake's gaze fell slightly—"I had to quiet you somehow. Those raiders, they take you off the stage?"

"Yes."

"Any of 'em around?"

Her eyes went back down the canyon.

"Down there," she said. "Through those rocks. By a creek."

"How far?"

She shook her head. "I don't know."

"How many?"

Addie looked up at him and swallowed.

"Five," she answered.

Jake nodded, then looked back at her a little shame-faced. "I'm sorry about that." He pointed at her jaw. "But I did have to do it. You just rest a minute, then we'll get movin'."

Jed Logan rode up the canyon at a half-gallop, and seeing that he was coming up and out of it, he slowed his horse, peering into the large boulders scattered through the wide entrance.

Nothing.

His eyes eased to the ground, combing through the gravel for some sign.

After moving over the ground for a few minutes he saw the fresh dirt where rocks had been knocked loose. The trail led up the canyon, into the rocks.

A slight smile pushed through his lips.

He would have her in a few minutes.

In the rocks, Jake reached out for the girl.

"Ma'am," he said.

Addie looked up.

"Best we move."

"Where?" she asked.

"Down the canyon, toward that creek."

Fear stiffened her face. "No," she shook her head. "Please . . ."

Jake raised his hand to calm her. "It'll be all right, ma'am. We—"

"No," she shook her head.

"Miss Ballard." Jake's voice hardened. "We need the water. Now—" His voice caught and he looked back down the canyon suddenly.

"What is it?" she asked.

Jake put his finger to his lips and motioned her down, then his head came up again, ears straining.

Hoofs clattered on rock faintly.

Hearing it, Addie flinched as if she'd been slapped. "No," she cried, and reeling, scrambling to her feet, she ran.

Bolting, Jake leaped to his feet, and reaching out, caught her by the waist, but she broke free running again.

"Sonofabitch," the hunter growled as he burst through the rocks, up toward the mouth. The girl was fast, faster than Jake would have figured. Plummeting through the rocks and around, she hurtled into the open, topping the rise, desperation exploding through her.

Below them, coming up the canyon, the man on horseback must have seen her, because Jake heard a whoop and the clatter of a horse running.

Pivoting, Jake saw the rider coming, cutting through the rocks, flickering fragment-like. He must not have seen Jake because he kept going for the girl, hammering up the sandstone, pounding up the mouth of the canyon and out into the open, closing on her.

Jake could see him clearly now. Fifty yards away. Driving for the woman, stringing a rope out in his hands.

Jake ran too. Charging across the tops of the boulders.

In the open, the man on horseback took a rope from his horn and swung it over his head, making a loop, then widened it. Riding hard, bearing down on the girl, he swished the loop over his head; closing in on her, he dropped the rope over her, and jerking it tight, he hauled her to the ground.

Addie struggled to get her feet under her, but Logan backed his horse, tautening the rope rigid, dragging her down again.

"Now you little bitch . . ." he whispered.

Behind him, Jake dropped to the ground, and measuring the distance between them, began running again.

Maybe sixty yards.

Stretching his legs out, Jake pulled for him, praying the

rider's attention would stay on the girl for a few more seconds. Just a few . . .

The man in the saddle snapped the rope again, raking the girl through the dirt.

Halting, he looked at her.

She didn't move this time.

Nodding, he wrapped the loose end of the rope around the horn and knotted it.

"That'll hold you," he growled, his eyes going back to her again. "Gonna teach you a lesson," he whispered, and lifting his leg to dismount, he heard something behind him. Running.

Half out of the saddle, he turned to see Jake pounding toward him.

Disbelief stunned him for a moment, holding him motionless. Watching Jake come.

Then his hand dropped to his gun, and he swung the horse around for a better shot. He had forgotten about the rope.

The horse's chest rammed into the rope holding the girl, and the animal crowhopped, reeling against the sudden restriction.

Jake saw the gun in the man's hand. He was trying to shoot and hold the horse at the same time and not having any luck.

The man in the saddle jerked off a shot, but the movement of the horse sent it wild.

Still running straight at the man, Jake slipped his knife from its leather. Not many men he knew threw their blade. Mainly because it was a damn poor way to use it.

But right now it was all he had.

The man in the saddle tore at his horse's head, struggling to use his gun-filled hand to free the rope from the horn, but his fingers were nearly useless and the movement kept ramming the animal into the rope, beginning to tangle his feet.

Logan must have realized he would never make it that

way because he fired once, then turned the horse away from Jake, trying to swing him in a circle and out of the rope.

And Jake threw.

The knife tumbled the twenty feet between them, catching the thin-faced man in the back of the shoulder. The blow wasn't a good one. The momentum of the knife carried the handle up and only the bare top of the blade sank into the flesh.

But it did its job.

Screaming, the thin-faced man pitched forward out of the saddle, crashing to the ground, the impact knocking the knife free.

Jake rushed at him.

Rolling in the dirt, the thin-faced man was turning, bringing his gun up and around.

Jake dove. Driving his elbow through the man's face, ramming them both into the ground, sending the pistol flying. Jake pounded down on his chest, crushing the air out of it like an old bellows. Getting his hands under him, pushing himself up, Jake could feel the man moving next to him, and reeling, Jake glanced a half-blow into the man's chest, and they both went into the dirt again.

For a moment, Jake was limboed in the heat, dust and sweat, and the caw of his breathing mixing with the other man's.

Swallowing air, Jake looked up, and only half saw the blow coming. More a slap than a punch, it landed on the side of his head, knocking him sprawling on his back.

Above him, the thin-faced man stumbled away, lunging for his horse. He fell short, but kept moving, pulling his legs under him like something very old, reaching out and grasping the stirrup, dragging himself to it.

And the rifle above it.

Jake rolled over on to all fours, his eyes searching for the pistol. Seeing it in the dirt, he jumped and fell on it.

Grasping the handle, he turned.

The thin-faced man had hauled himself up beside the horse, his hand on the rifle butt, yanking it from its boot.

Jake lifted the pistol, centering it on the man's chest as he freed the rifle, turning.

And shot him three times.

Kneeling beside the stream, Canfield's eyes came up suddenly.

"Shot," he whispered; then standing, staring back down the canyon, he waited to be sure.

Another thump dotted the air, and turning from the water, he ran back up the hill.

"Phil," he yelled, kicking at the sleeping man's boots, waking him.

The big-shouldered man sat up, bleary-eyed. "What the hell, you—"

"Shots," Canfield snapped, and turned to the others. They were rousing too.

All but Logan.

"Jed," he whispered, then turned to Sidy. He had been beside him.

"Where is he?"

The old man shrugged. "I dunno, I—"

An echo of gunfire drifted toward them. Distant. Nearly soft.

"What's that?" the old man asked.

Canfield looked to the horses. Logan's was gone.

"I don't know," Canfield said, running for the horses. "But I'm gonna find out."

# TWELVE

The roar of the shots seemed to linger in the dusty air as Jake walked to where his knife had fallen and picked it up. Stepping across the body, he went to the horse and cut the rope holding the girl. Leaning on the horse, he looked out to her. She was still on the ground.

"You all right?" he called.

Her head came up, then bobbed soundlessly.

"Miss?"

"Yes," she answered. "I'm all right."

Nodding, Jake pushed away from the horse and leaned over the dead man. Unbuckling his gun belt, Jake jerked it free and hung it over his shoulder, then moved down to the dead man's feet and yanked his boots off. With the boots in one hand, he picked the man's hat up, gathered in the horse's reins, and walked out to the girl.

She was on her feet now. Shaken, but on them.

"So far you've had a rough day," he said.

The girl looked up at him.

"Take these," Jake said, holding out the hat and boots to her.

Her eyes fell to them blankly.

"Take 'em," Jake insisted, forcing them into her hands. "And get up on the horse. Those shots are goin' to bring his friends, and we're gonna need to be someplace else when they get here."

She looked back at the man in the dust.

"Is he dead?"

"Yes'm," Jake nodded, a frown weighting his mouth. "He's dead."

Then looking up, he brought the horse around, motioning her up. "Now," he barked. "Let's go."

Blinking and putting the hat on her head, Addie placed her foot in the stirrup and Jake helped her on board.

She looked back at Logan again.

"He . . . tried to force me . . ." she whispered.

"Ain't gonna do nothin' no more," Jake said, and turning, began leading the horse.

"No," Addie murmured. "No."

Then the motion of the horse took her. And they were running.


Walt Canfield and his men came up out of the canyon slowly, their guns drawn and ready.

Over the rise, and into the open space.

"Walt," Taylor said, pointing.

Canfield saw it at almost the same time. A sprawl of color in the mute dust.

"Yeah," he nodded. "Fan," he said, and the men spread out on both sides of him; riding in a horizontal line, they eased across the flat.

The sprawl of color gained form. Becoming the twist of a dead man.

"Jesus," Taylor murmured as they came up on the body and reined their horses in.

The muscles in Canfield's jaw trembled.

"Howie, you and Rem take a look around," he ordered them.

The two men turned their horses out and Canfield and Gage dismounted.

"Walt," Gage pointed out. "His boots are gone."

"Yeah," Canfield nodded. "I saw that. So's his gun belt. See if his gun's around anyplace."

Gage's eyes roamed over the ground as Canfield knelt down beside Logan. The dead man was lying on his side, his shoulder slumped over his face. Reaching down to turn him over, Canfield saw the wound in his back.

"Knife," he said, and lifting the shoulder he turned Logan over.

Frowning, Gage turned back to Canfield. "I don't see his gun nowhere." His eyes rested on Logan. "Damn . . ." he sighed. "Poor old Jed."

"He was stupid," Canfield said, then looked up as Sidy rode back in.

"Sent Howie on out a ways," he said dismounting, and looked at Canfield. "Far as I can tell it's just one fella. And he's got the girl with him. And somethin' kind of funny . . ." he added. "I can't find no horse tracks but Jed's."

Canfield looked up. "You mean he was on foot?"

"Looks like."

"Jesus," Canfield shook his head. "On foot and using a knife."

"Yeah," Sidy nodded. "Who you figger it is?"

Canfield walked around the body and a little way out. He shook his head. "Beats the hell out of me."

"Law, maybe," Gage ventured.

"Maybe," Canfield allowed slowly. "But what the hell's he doin' on foot?"

"Yeah," the thick-shouldered man frowned, shrugging. "Somebody from back at the stage stop, maybe?"

"That's the best bet," Canfield agreed. "But I don't think so. They were all dead." He shook his head. "Dammit," he growled. "I had it all covered—"

"Hell," Sidy laughed, cutting in. "'Member 'long when I was a youngster 'bout Howie's age, we was gonna hit a train. Put the stationmaster down in a root cellar. When the train come along we was gonna signal it like the stationmaster. Trouble was the sonofabitch dug his way out and got the drop on us. That's when I done my first spell in Yuma—"

Canfield listened impatiently, then barked, "What the hell you gettin' at, Rem?"

Sidy looked at him blankly. "Dunno," he shrugged. "Just the same sorta thing. No such thing as havin' it made, I guess."

Canfield stared at the old outlaw.

"You know, Rem," he said finally, "for somebody that ain't too bright, you amaze me sometimes."

"No," the old man sniffed, "I ain't too bright." Straightening, he looked at Canfield. "But I ain't no fool neither. I've lived awhile to prove that."

A nervous smile touched Canfield's lips as he looked at the old man like a dark reflection.

"Howie," Gage pointed, and looking up, Canfield watched the youngster come back down the mouth of the canyon.

"Nothin'," the young man called. "Headed back north," he said as he rode in and dismounted.

"You sure?" Canfield asked.

Taylor nodded.

"Damn," the leader sighed, perplexed.

Gage rubbed his chin.

"Maybe it was just the girl he was after," he offered.

"Yeah," Canfield said doubtfully.

"Maybe he—" Sidy started.

"Or maybe he was a ghost," Canfield exploded, then contained his anger, looking back up the canyon. "Or maybe he wasn't here at all. Come on," he frowned, and turning back down the hill, he walked to his horse. "We're wastin' time here," he said, mounting up. "We got an appointment to keep."

The others mounted, and as they rode out, Canfield hesitated, looking back at Logan, then up the canyon.

A tightness began gathering in his chest and he felt his breathing thicken.

"I had it covered," he swallowed. "I—"

Behind him, Rem Sidy yelled back at him. "Hey, Walt, you comin'—"

Canfield looked back at the old man. Waiting. The others

had drawn up too. Their eyes on him. He felt suddenly exposed.

"Yeah," he said, tearing his horse's head around, spurring him hard. "Let's go."

# THIRTEEN

Jake ran.

Leading the horse, he jogged back the way he'd come, then swinging into the saddle in front of Addie, he angled off, coming in wide to the rim of the canyon.

Dismounting, he tied the horse to a stunted juniper and looked back at the girl in the saddle.

She was still dazed, hovering on the edge of shock.

"Miss—" he said.

Blinking, she raised her eyes.

"You all right?"

"Yes," she said. "Fine."

"Might as well get down," Jake suggested.

"Why?"

"I'm gonna go up there and see if I can spot them fellas."

Her eyes widened slightly. "You think they might be near?"

Jake shook his head, "I don't know," he answered. "That's what I need to find out." He held his hand out. "Come on down now, rest a bit."

She looked at his hand, and ignoring it, lowered herself to the ground, and sat on a small outcropping.

Jake shrugged, then looked up the ridge. "I'm goin' up there," he pointed.

The girl stood up, the fear in her eyes again. "You're leaving?"

"Only for a couple of minutes. You'll be able to see me."

Nodding, she sat down again. "All right," she whispered.

"Nothin' to worry about," Jake said, and turning, he started up the long rise.

The morning sun pressed into him, and climbing, he began to feel some fatigue. He had gotten used to walking. Riding had let him know how tired he was.

Ignoring the weariness, he went on to the top, and coming up on the crest, he knelt down, then stretched out.

His eyes moved back the way he'd come. Slowly measuring the hills and arroyos coming toward him, trying to pick movement off the skylines and out of the cuts in the earth. He frowned. Nothing. No dust, no nothing between him and the opening of that canyon. And they had had plenty of time to get there and come after them.

He eased his gaze back down the canyon, thinking they might have—

His eyes stopped. Deep in the canyon, a dot spiraled into the air. Then another. Drifting. Quail. Jake nodded.

They had gone back down the canyon.

Jake sat up, his eyes narrowing, perplexed. Away, and not after them. He thought about it another minute, then knowing he was doing no good, he shrugged and walked back down the ridge.

The girl's eyes jerked up as Jake bottomed the incline and walked back to her.

"They've gone back down the canyon," he said.

"Back?"

Jake frowned. "Yeah. You say they took you off the stage for ransom?"

She nodded. "Yes. They're from Mexico. They wanted the money for guns."

Jake thought for a moment, then shook his head. "Somethin' ain't sittin' right here."

"You mean because they didn't come after us?"

Jake nodded. "Yeah."

Addie shrugged. "They might have thought you were a posse after me. Something like that."

"Could be," Jake acknowledged grudgingly. "Where were they headed?"

Addie shook her head. "The leader, Canfield, said the less I knew the better."

Jake nodded. "Smart man. Less everybody knows the better. That way nobody can get ahead of him. He the one wearin' the old campaign hat?"

"Yes."

"Ex-army man most likely," Jake guessed. "Probably . . ."

"Mr. Hooker," Addie cut in, "I don't see what it matters now. It's over with and we can start back now."

Jake's eyes came up. "No, miss," he said. "We can't. We're goin' after 'em."

Addie blinked. "What?"

"We're goin' after 'em," Jake repeated.

"Why?"

"They stole some money from me," Jake explained. "My stake for Australia."

Realization crept into her eyes. "You didn't come after me, then?"

Jake cleared his throat. "Well, no, I didn't. Look," he said, sitting her down, "there's a trading post up ahead. Miller's. I'll leave you there."

"I want to get back. I've got to get to school. Isn't there anyplace closer?"

"Well," Jake thought. "Place south of here maybe."

"Then why don't you take me there?"

"Because," Jake answered, "I ain't got the time. And right now time is everything."

"I'll just slow you up, Mr. Hooker. Can't you—"

"Look," Jake snapped, then pressed his anger back. "There's two ways of huntin'. By figurin' and by scent."

"Scent—?"

"Trackin'," Jake explained, then went on. "Now these fellas have done somethin' that don't make sense to me. That means I can't try and outfigure 'em—I have to go by scent alone. I go takin' you off somewhere, I might lose them and my money."

She glared at him. "If your money is so damned important, my father can pay you."

Frowning, Jake stood again. "I don't take money I ain't earned. We gotta get movin'." He turned to the horse and opened the saddlebags. "Most likely this fella had a change of clothes—"

"I will not wear men's clothes," Addie announced, standing up.

Jake turned and faced her. "Miss Ballard," he said quietly, "I don't like it any better'n you. But you're goin' with me. And that dress ain't gonna do for travelin'. Now you're gonna change and—"

"And don't tell me what I have to do."

"Yes," he nodded, "I will. Now you're either gonna change or I'm gonna leave you right where you stand."

She blinked. "You wouldn't dare."

"Don't bet on it. That money's what I'm out here for and that's what I'm gonna get." Reaching into the saddlebags, he pulled out a pair of jeans and a shirt. He threw them to her, and they landed at her feet. Picking up the boots and hat, he tossed them too. "It's up to you."

She glared at him.

"You're a brutish, hairy, mean old sonofabitch."

"And I can outcuss you if you want to get into that. I'm leavin' here in about two minutes. You comin' or not?"

She stood unmoving.

Shrugging, Jake started to turn to the horse.

"All right," she burst out, and gathering up the clothes, she went behind the rocks.

Turning back to the horse, he shook his head wearily.

He had to give her one thing. She was right. He would be better off without her.

"Damn," he sighed. His luck was running from bad to worse. Not only did he have to follow the raiders but he had to contend with her. The last thing he needed at this point was somebody else to worry about. And a damned female at that. To Jake she ranked somewhere between being in hell with his back broke and having a horse sit on him.

He mulled several ways of getting rid of her, then gave them all up, shaking his head.

Those fellas had taken away any element of choice he might have had.

All he could do was follow. And take her along. Sighing acceptingly, he knew he'd better get to it, and the first thing he needed to do was take stock of what he had.

Opening the saddlebags, he began going through them. Another shirt. Dried beef jerky, which he bit into. Three boxes of shells. A folded-up picture of a girl in her underwear from a Sears Roebuck catalogue. Jake examined that for a moment as he chewed on the jerky; then nodding approvingly, he folded it up and slipped it in his shirt pocket. Probing into the bags again, his fingers touched something hard. Wrapped in oilcloth. He pulled it out and unwrapped it. It was an old Colt Peacemaker. Jake smiled. He liked it better than the new automatic in the holster. He tested the action, then shoved it in his belt. He was stuffing the shirt and cloth back in the bags when he heard the girl's steps behind him.

Turning, he smiled almost automatically, which was a mistake.

"Am I that amusing?" she snapped. The clothes were too big and hung on her. The hat was lopsided and she shuffled in the oversized boots. But there was something about her—

"Well—"

Jake shook his head. "No," he said, and turning, he slipped the canteen free and lifted it over the saddle. He unscrewed the top and handed it to her. Approaching, she took it and drank, then handed it back.

Jake took it and took a short swig. "You know, little bit," he said, "when someone smiles at you, it don't mean they're lookin' to fight you."

"My name is Addie. Miss Ballard."

Jake smiled, nodding. "Well, Miss Ballard. You can call

me Mr. Hooker." He started to turn to the horse, then looked at her. "And I hope that spunk ain't just too much air. You're gonna need it."

With Addie behind him, Jake rode down the canyon, went wide of where he knew Logan's body was, then headed toward the creek.

As they neared it, Jake could feel the girl behind him tensing, and when they reached it, her arms were tight around him.

Dismounting, he moved over the ground, kneeling beside the prints in the mud beside the water.

"Two, three hours," he nodded, and standing again, he looked up at the girl. "Stand down for a minute," he said. "Wash your face or somethin', while I get fresh water. Do you good."

"I don't like it here," she said.

"We ain't gonna be here that long," Jake said, taking the canteen down from the saddle horn. "Come on now—"

"Quit giving me orders—"

"Goddammit, little bit," he snapped, "will you quit givin' me so goddamn much trouble? You're not doin' any good gettin' your rile up against me. I'm on your side."

Addie didn't flinch. She looked down at him. "Are you, Mr. Hooker? Like everybody else, I think you're only on your own."

Jake stared up at her for a moment, then shaking his head, grumbling, he walked down to the creek and filled the canteen.

Five minutes later, they were moving again.

They rode in silence. Jake didn't know whether to try and talk to her or just let it go. He'd never been around women that much, much less one like this. Spoiled contrary, a chip on her shoulder, and a line of defense a buffalo gun wouldn't pierce.

He wished Pike were there right now. All that talking he

did about people not bein' so bad. Jake wanted to saddle him
with this one for about ten minutes and see what he said.

Although, Jake admitted quietly to himself, Pike was right
about some things . . .

His family for one.

Memory twisted in him. Stark and cold. Nearly making
him shiver. An echo like a flash of light. But that's all there
was. That's all he ever let it be. He never let himself go too
near it, or think about it.

He'd never even told anybody about it. Only Pike once
when he was drunk, and then only a part of it.

Yet it was always there. Just beyond the edge of consciousness. Pursuing him. His mother and father reaching for
help. The rifle being leveled on him—

He shook his head, forcing it away.

He made himself think of Australia. And all that space.
Empty and free.

Under him, Jake felt the horse pulling upward, and lifting his eyes, Jake saw they were coming up and out of the
canyon.

Jake frowned. He had been thinking a long time.

"Gettin' mush-headed," he grumbled.

"What?"

His eyes jerked around at the girl as if she were an in-
truder. He'd forgotten she was there.

"Nothin'," he said curtly.

She looked at him. "Do you talk to yourself, Mr. Hooker?"

"I been known to," he answered, his eyes dropping to the
ground, trying to pick out the raider's tracks.

"You could go crazy doing that," she said.

He turned and looked at her. "Right now that would come
in second," he said.

"What do you mean by that?"

Jake frowned. "Miss Ballard, I ain't out here to jaw to you.
I got other things to do."

His eyes went back to the ground, and picking up the

tracks, he followed them out of the canyon into a narrow rock valley.

"No need to be rude," she said after a moment.

"Miss Ballard," he sighed, "I ain't tryin' to be rude. I ain't tryin' to do nothin' but catch up with them fellas."

They started down into the valley.

Addie was quiet for a moment, then said, "This place you want to go—"

"Australia."

"Why is it so important?"

"Because," Jake said, kicking the horse out, "it's all I got left."

# FOURTEEN

Canfield and his men rode until twilight, then made camp on high ground.

Unable to eat, Canfield moved to the edge of the firelight, slipping a cigar from his vest. Putting a match to it, he looked back the way he'd come.

The night was shadow-clear, a black crystal substance weaving itself into a dark mirror. He could see it, nearly touched it, but he could not enter. And somewhere in the mirror, he could feel a fragment pressing toward him—

"That fella?"

Canfield's eyes pulled around as Phil Gage approached him.

"What?"

Gage pointed into the darkness. "That fella still on your mind?"

Canfield brought his eyes back around slowly. "He's like an itch. A cog out of sync that throws ever' thing else off."

"Logic," Gage said.

Canfield nodded. "Exactly."

"Some things ain't logical," Gage offered.

Canfield shook his head. "No, there are just unknown elements. In this case the why. Everything is ordered, Phil. Once you know that order you've got the advantage, an edge. Fella said once if you gave him a lever and the right place to put it, he could move the earth, and it's true. All you need is that edge." Canfield puffed his cigar. "Once I know what this fella's why is, I'll know how to move him."

"What about until then?"

Canfield frowned. "Until then I've got a bare edge and that ain't much. If he comes after us he's got to follow us because he don't know where we're goin'. And if he follows, I can lead him where I want him."

"And if he don't?"

Canfield looked at him. "He will," he nodded, tossing the cigar away. "He has to," he whispered, turning and walking back up into the camp.

Sidy and Taylor were playing cards. Canfield knelt beside the fire and poured a cup of coffee, watching them for a moment, then stood again restlessly.

"You're cheatin'," Taylor said.

"Now why would I want to cheat you? We ain't even playin' for money," Sidy pointed out. He looked up at Canfield. "You wanna join in, boss?"

Canfield glanced down at the old man. "No," he said, and flinging the coffee away, dropped the cup and went to his saddlebags. Opening them, he took out a curry comb and brush, then strode down to the horses.

"What the hell's with him?" he heard Sidy wonder behind him.

Walking in beside his horse, he began to curry him hard and fast, stopping for a moment to take off his hat and place it on a rock, then working with the comb and brush again with hard swift strokes.

He worked methodically, wishing the system and the rhythm would push all thought from his mind.

It didn't.

The man behind them seemed to be even more with him.

Hesitating, Canfield straightened up, and leaning against his horse, he looked into the darkness, then shook his head. He had planned it all out. And planning—doing it by the book—was everything.

His eyes slipped to his old hat.

He had learned it the hard way a long time ago. Fifteen years ago now in a place called Cuba.

Fifteen years and a lot of wars ago.

His eyes lingered on the hat like a visible memory.

He had been issued the hat, along with the rest of his first lieutenant's uniform, just before he had landed in Cuba to fight the Spanish.

He smiled, remembering. First Lieutenant Walter Laine Canfield. Another in the long line of Cavalry Canfields.

Those first days had been good ones. Full of dash and glory. Just the way he'd dreamed it would be. And as it should be in dreams he was decorated for bravery, promoted in the field, and given his own command.

His mouth thinned and his hands tightened on the comb and brush. Then the dream ended one day in early spring, when he had been given orders to burn a small town on the coast. The expedient thing to do, his commander, Colonel Benton, told him. The town was believed to be a stronghold for the Spanish and Spanish sympathizers. The company was moving fast, going on ahead, and Canfield had been given the assignment.

Canfield rode into the village with his detail. The mayor, a small gray man, met him in the square and begged him not to do it. It was all they had, he pleaded. Canfield looked at the people as the mayor spoke. Poor people. Dirty, hungry, and tired.

And Canfield listened to the mayor. Mounting his horse, and leading his men out, he had left the town behind, still standing. The brass would never know, Canfield reasoned, they were moving so fast, one town more or less didn't matter.

Canfield tried to catch up with the rest of the company, but was still ten miles behind them when darkness came.

He called camp in a small clearing in the jungle. They had eaten and just taken to their bedrolls when he heard the first scream.

Bolting up out of his blankets, he saw a swarm of shadows rushing from the trees, sweeping over his men. He was turning, reaching for his gun, when a bullet hit him in the shoulder, knocking him into the brush, and he passed out.

When he came to, he found himself completely covered

with brush. Turning onto his stomach, he could see into the clearing. The half-light from the fire fluttered over the bodies, an occasional shot thumping the air. Then one of the shadows ebbed through the light, his face clear for a moment.

It was the mayor who had pleaded with Canfield.

Canfield raised up, trying to crawl, trying to get to him, but the movement drained him, and slumping, he passed out again.

When he awoke he was in a field hospital. Colonel Benton arrived an hour later. He told Canfield coldly that he had two choices: resign for the good of the service or be court-martialed.

Canfield begged for another chance, but Benton just shook his head.

"You go by the book," Benton said, "or it breaks you."

By the book.

Putting the comb and brush into one hand, he came around the horse and picked up the hat gently.

He had resigned and was out of the Cavalry a week later.

Now he had a chance to get it all back. If the mission came off well, there could be a place on the general's staff. And one piece out of place was getting in the way of it.

One fluke.

His hand tightened on the tools.

Going by the book had gotten him through fifteen years. Living by logic alone.

It was the only way he knew. The only way back.

And if the man back there came after them it would work against him.

It had to.

# FIFTEEN

Walking, leading the horse with the girl aboard, Jake followed the tracks until all the light was gone.

Finally he pulled up and stood for a moment, his breath stretching through him like a razored wire, fatigue heavy in his back and legs, and the need for sleep pressing through him like a part of the darkness.

He could go on, but he needed the rest. He had to admit that; he didn't like it, but it was true. Getting old.

Then there was the girl.

"Are we stopping, Mr. Hooker?" she asked.

Jake glanced around. "Yeah," he nodded. "This is as good as any."

"Good," she sighed, and slipped down from the saddle. "Some hot food will taste good."

"Yeah," Jake agreed. "It would."

She looked at him. "Would?"

"Well"—Jake pushed his hair back and scratched his beard—"for one thing we ain't got no food but some jerky and coffee—"

"Coffee, then."

"And for another thing," Jake went on, "we ain't buildin' no fires."

The girl stared at him. "No fire!" she exclaimed. "I'm cold and some coffee would be good."

"No fire," Jake repeated. "Those fellas are on higher ground than we are. They might spot it. And right now all we got goin' for us is the fact that they don't know where we are."

She stared at him a moment. "How about blankets? Or do you think they might smell them?"

A smile tugged Jake's lips. "I've seen some they could. No, miss," he said, turning to the horse. "You can have 'em both."

"No," she said. "I'll take one. There's no need for false gallantry, Mr. Hooker."

Jake untied the blankets, and taking them off the saddle, handed them to her.

"Not that," he said. "Just I don't need 'em. Ain't that cold to me. I like the feel of the air."

"Mr. Hooker, I know you don't like me. You don't have to—"

"It ain't that I don't like you, Miss Ballard. You just don't make it real easy *to* like you."

He turned back to the saddlebags and pulled out strands of jerky and handed her one. Walking to a rock, he sat down in front of it and leaned back on its face, taking a chew of the dried meat.

"It's all right," Jake said. "Tastes pretty good and it'll swell up when you get it down. Fill you up."

"I can imagine," Addie said, sitting down on the blanket roll and biting reluctantly into her piece. She chewed for a long time and swallowed. "People who eat this must stay very healthy just from the exercise."

Jake smiled. "That's a part of its lure."

Addie looked down at the jerky.

"When I get back to school," she said, "I'm going to have the cook make me the biggest roast and potatoes in the world."

Jake's eyes eased up, studying her for a moment. "How 'bout home? Ain't you gonna go home first?"

Her eyes faded. "No," she answered.

"Imagine your folks'll want to see you."

She shook her head. "I don't have any parents, not the way you mean. There is only my father."

"He's folks ain't he?"

"We're related, if that's what you mean."

Jake hesitated, biting off another chew. "You don't sound too fond of him."

A slight frown weighted the corners of her mouth. "It's not that," she said almost softly, then stiffened. "I don't feel very much for him one way or another."

Jake stopped chewing, the amazement widening his eyes.

"You gonna sit there an' tell me you don't care nothin' for your own pa?"

"He's just a person."

Jake blinked. "He's your family," he said quietly.

A mixture of frustration and anger exploded in the girl's eyes. "You're so damned stupid I doubt if you'd understand."

"Somethin' like that don't take understandin'."

"Just because somebody is your father is no reason to love him."

"Now that is stupid," Jake snapped. "Where the hell'd you come across thinkin' like that, in that school?"

"There," she nodded, "and from my father."

"Your pa—"

"Who do you think sent me to the school in the first place, Mr. Hooker? To get rid of me. Some time ago he realized I wasn't going to be pretty, that I was going to be an old maid. I was an embarrassment to him. It doesn't look good, you know, for a successful man to have a failure as an offspring. And a woman who is not beautiful, not married, is a failure. So he sent me to school. The best school."

Jake thought for a moment. "Might'a been—" he began.

Addie cut him off, "No. You were going to give him a nice reason for doing it, but there isn't one. People do what's best for them. No, Mr. Hooker, we all do what we have to in order to survive. We're all alone."

The last words brought Jake's eyes up suddenly. It was like seeing a part of him set aside so he could look at it. In him it seemed natural, but in the girl it was misshapen.

Jake blinked. "Felt that way some myself," he allowed,

and pushed the last of his jerky in his mouth. "Time we was beddin' down—" He eased back against a rock.

"You haven't lived much around people have you, Mr. Hooker?" Addie asked.

Jake looked at her. "No. Mountains, mostly."

She nodded. "You're lucky. I wish I could do something like that. Be rid of people."

Jake stared at her, then leaned back again, closing his eyes. "Night, Miss Ballard," he said.

"Good night, Mr. Hooker."

Jake could hear her laying out her blankets, then she was quiet. Opening his eyes, he looked at her, an ache kindling in him like the whisper of a forgotten song. A pain of time and distance and an old fear.

# SIXTEEN

Addie slept fitfully and the morning came before she was ready for it. It seemed like she hadn't slept at all.

Trembling in the morning chill, she sat up stiffly and looked where Jake had been sitting.

He was gone.

Jerking upright, her eyes raced over the small area. The horse was still there.

A flicker of movement up the hill pulled her eyes around. Jake Hooker topped the rise and ambled down toward her, holding something in his hands.

"Mornin'," he nodded, crossing to her. Kneeling down, in front of her, he held out a handful of red berries. "Foragin'" he explained.

Addie looked at the fruit doubtfully, then back to Jake.

"Buffalo berries," he said, pushing them toward her, and at the same time put one in his mouth. "Do your stomach some good. Get somethin' fresh in it, 'sides that jerky."

She took one hesitantly. It tasted tart and sweet at the same time, drawing the muscles in her jaw and throat.

"Go on," Jake said. "Least they ain't summer berries. They're enough to make a bear grin."

Addie ate another, then another.

"Couple more," Jake said. "And a bit of jerky. Don't want to eat too many of 'em. They give you the—" He stopped himself.

Addie's eyes lifted. "What?"

Jake shrugged, "Oh, they . . . give you an upset stomach sometimes."

Addie felt the tug of a smile.

"And diarrhea," she added.

"What's that?"

"The polite word for what you were about to say."

"Oh," Jake sniffed. "Don't know too many of them nice words. Never had much learnin'."

"You never went to school?"

Jake looked up. "Some," he replied.

"But everyone should have a good education. Your parents should have—"

"Leave my folks out of this," Jake snapped suddenly.

Addie blinked at his abrupt change. "Really, Mr. Hooker, there's no need to be angry, I was just going to say—"

"Don't matter," Jake said. "It ain't none of your concern." He turned to the horse before she could say anything. "Time we was leavin'," he announced, tossing the berries away.

"Mr. Hooker," the girl sputtered. "Do you mean you're going to walk away right in the middle of a discussion?"

"That what we're havin', a discussion?"

"Yes."

"Be damned," he shrugged. "Guess I am then."

Watching him walk away, Addie felt like throwing something at him. He was so damn stubborn. Never anything but rude and nasty. Except for that moment she'd mentioned his parents, she remembered. Then he'd been different. Almost vulnerable.

And for that moment, she'd almost liked him.

Almost.

Canfield and his men rode hard through the morning, through small rugged hills, then up onto the level ground on a small plateau.

By mid-morning the sun burned down on them from the cloudless blue sky, and they began to leave the flat ground. Down a narrow valley and up its far wall, lifting into the foothills. A scattering of grass began in the hills, mingling with a few scrub piñon pine.

Reaching the crest of the valley, Canfield pulled his horse in.

"Take a couple," he said, standing down. He turned to his horse, and lifting the stirrup to adjust his cinch, he looked back the way they'd come.

The heat latticed the air in colorless blendings. The horses' hoofs scraped on rock, mingling with the crunch of their grazing and a few tired words from the men.

The heat seemed to catch things in motion. Stealing movement from them. Birds hovering skyward caught in a gravity lulling them away from the earth, limboed with the men's voices.

Canfield's horse shifted his weight and Canfield was about to bring his eyes around when a pin point of light blinked and was gone.

He turned away from the horse. Waiting. Nothing but space and voices and heat. But he knew it had been there.

Nodding, his stomach trembled and he dropped the stirrup and mounted up.

"Start looking for a place," he said to Gage.

The thick-shouldered man squinted questioningly in the sunlight. "What?"

"Start lookin' for a place," Canfield said again. "I was right. He's still back there. And still comin'."

Canfield led them up the hills, purposely staying to the middle ground, going as straight as possible, but taking his time.

Gage glanced back over the trail.

"He might lose it," he pointed out.

Canfield nodded. "Could be, but I doubt it. I make it too easy for him, he's gonna know he's walkin' into a trap."

Gage looked back again, then shook his head. "I don't know, Walt," he said doubtfully. "We're wastin' a lot of time. We miss Hoffer—"

"We're not gonna miss him," Canfield said.

Gage pulled his eyes around. "We might," he snapped. "We can outrun this fella if—"

"Maybe," he allowed. "But I don't like people at my back. Not good tactics. He caught up with us once. He could do it again. And when he does, I want it to be on my terms, not his."

They came around the shoulder of a hill and down into a wide, fast-running stream lined with cottonwoods and a few aspen.

"Let 'em drink," Canfield said to the others, and they stopped along the water; then he raised his eyes to the hills breathing into mountains.

"Not long," he said, and lifting his horse's head, they started out again.

They followed the stream up, through hills that steepened to a rim on the far side and became wooded on theirs. They came to a small falls, and fording on top of it, rode up a break on the far steep side. They made their way along the break to the rim, then through a park of pine and aspen, and up another incline across open ground toward a sharp bluff above them.

Canfield drew his horse in, his eyes moving over the open area, then to the bluff. It was steep; fifty feet of rocky, sparsely wooded ground with a forty-five degree angle down the incline from the top.

He looked back down the slope. The scrub pine and aspen lined the rim, then fanned up the incline to the left until they nearly touched the bottom bluff. It was cut off by a spine of sandstone that made a natural trail to the top.

"Good spot," Gage commented.

Canfield nodded. "All but those trees down there," he said, and nudged his horse out. He followed the spine to the top of the bluff, then to its highest point.

Looking back down, he smiled. The line of fire was clear.

Anybody riding into that clearing would be a prime target.

"Yeah," he nodded, pulling his rifle from its boot. "Here."

Jake and Addie came across the plateau, down a small valley, then up it again, climbing toward the hills.

"They stopped here," Jake said, slowing the horse and

pointing over the ground. His eyes lifted from the ground to the mountains. "Still headed for Miller's it looks like," he thought aloud, and nudged the horse out again.

His eyes went back to the ground.

The tracks were even and clean, regularly spaced. Moving slower, he noted. Almost easy—

Jake stopped, suddenly looking around in reflex, his eyes picking over the hills.

Behind him, Addie leaned out, looking at his face.

"Something wrong, Mr. Hooker?"

Jake glanced back at her, then scanning the ground again, shook his head.

"Gettin' spooked, I guess."

"Why?"

"Trail," he explained, gesturing at the hoofmarks in the dirt. "Different since we came off the hill."

"How?"

"Regular," he said. "Too regular. Like they're takin' their time."

"Maybe they are."

"Yeah," Jake allowed grudgingly, then looked back at her. "If anything does happen," he said, "get behind somethin' first, then try and keep hold of the horse. And do 'em in that order, understand."

Addie stiffened. "You're giving me orders again, Mr. Hooker."

"That's right, Miss Ballard. I'm also tryin' to keep you from gettin' your rear shot off. No apology for the language."

"I'll watch out for my own 'rear,' thank you. No apology for the language."

"Then think about mine," he said, turning front, nudging the horse to movement.

They traveled for another hour, and rounding the thrust of a hill, they came down to a wide, fast-running stream.

Dismounting, Jake knelt down beside the water, and letting the horse push his muzzle into the water, Jake joined him. The water was cold and sweet. It tasted like the mountains, hurting his teeth and wiping a swath through the dust.

He pulled his face up, his own muzzle dripping, and he laughed.

"Better'n a bath," he sighed, and cupping his hands, he dragged the water up, pushing it across his face and through his matted hair.

Behind him, Addie stepped down from the horse.

"Nothing is better than a hot bath, Mr. Hooker," she said, and started upstream.

Jake looked around at her, the water cool on his face. He felt the anger twist in him, then he shrugged it away.

"That's town clean, ma'am. Ain't what I'm talking about."

Pausing, Addie looked back around at him. "Town clean? Clean is clean."

Standing, Jake smiled. "No, ma'am, it ain't. There's always more'n one way to things. Like clean to a mountain man, or an Indian. And clean to a white man. White man tries his damnedest not to smell like he does natural. Like an animal. Hunters do everything they can to smell like an animal so the other animals won't notice them so much. And the Indians. I always stood in woodsmoke to perfume myself when I lived in the mountains. Wore bear fur so's I could winter there. No," he shook his head, "it's like most ever'thin' else. It's all in the way you think about it."

Addie stared up at him, then blinked. "You sure you've hardly been to school?"

Jake's lips tugged. "Books ain't the only way to learn."

She shook her head. "It's just to look at you . . ." Her face reddened and she realized what she'd said and stammered. "I mean—"

Jake's grin darkened, fading. "I know what you mean, miss. Most folks look at this rough old boy, and they think the brain must be rough too."

Her gaze fell. "Yes," she said. "I'm familiar with that kind of thinking."

Jake felt a sudden softness for her. "Point is," he said, "don't mean nothin'."

"Some people put a great deal of worth in beauty," she said quietly. "Women especially. Their whole identity is tied up with how beautiful they are, because that's how men evaluate them." She looked up, her eyes oddly clouded. "But of course, that's ridiculous." She turned back to the stream, dipping her hands in the water, deliberately putting her back to Jake.

"Other kinds of worth . . ." Jake began, and saw that she wasn't going to answer. The distance was there again. A duality of motion in her. A strength from weakness, and a weakness in her strength. A fragile web like Jake remembered seeing in the trees once, morning bright, chained with dew. Changing color with every step he took. Strong only in its small realm. Unable to touch or be touched.

A twist of frustration ached through his stomach, and Jake wished there was something he could do, then was angry at her for making him feel that way. It was none of his concern.

"Hell," he sighed, turning back to the horse. He had other things to do. He couldn't spend time worrying about one hardheaded, contrary female.

"Come on," he snapped. "We gotta be movin'."

Sitting against a rock, trying to get some shade, his rifle in his hand, Canfield lifted the brim of his hat and looked at the sun.

An hour, he figured, and wiped the sweat from his neck.

The sun was like a hammer on the naked rocks.

His eyes moved to Taylor keeping watch.

"Anything?" he asked.

The young man looked at him and slowly shook his head.

"Hellava place to wait for somebody," Sidy grumbled shifting weight and rubbing his right leg.

Canfield looked at him. "Relieve the boy," he said to Sidy.

The old man's eyes came up. "Now?"

Canfield frowned. "If I told you to jump off a train track with the train comin' you'd ask, 'Now?' Yes, now, goddammit."

"I was just gettin' comfortable. Leg's been—"

"Howie's been out there an hour. Now get to it."

Grumbling under his breath, the old man got up, and carrying his rifle, he emerged into the sun squinting. "You're spelled," he said to the younger man, then sat down, trying to get his butt and right leg on the rocks.

"And keep your eyes downslope," Canfield barked. "Jesus," he sighed, easing back against the rocks, slipping his hat back down over his eyes.

# SEVENTEEN

With Addie riding behind, Jake followed the tracks up the stream, around a small falls, then up along a rim rising above the stream.

Forcing the girl from his mind, he made himself concentrate on the tracks. They were still clear, and that began to gnaw at him again.

"If it's not one thing it's another," he grumbled.

"What?"

He glanced back. "Nothin'," he frowned.

"Are you talking to yourself again?"

"No," he answered. "The horse." His eyes returned to the ground, and he slowed the animal, then stopped, looking up and around through the thickening brush and trees.

The sound of the stream rushed below the rim, and the sun was fragmented by the trees into hot shards. The tracks went through the pine, then straight up a steep incline, and around a bluff of broken rocks and trees.

His eyes moved over the bluff.

"Mr. Hooker?"

"Not now—"

"I was just—"

"Jesus H. Christ," Jake sighed wearily, looking back around at her. "Will you leave me be for a minute?"

"What are we doing?"

"You're askin' a lot of questions, and I'm tryin' to get rid of a bad feelin'." He looked back up the slope. He examined the slope for nearly a full minute, then shook his head. "It don't sit right," he said. "Those first tracks this mornin' showed they were in a hurry, then up on top of that valley, they slowed down. Now," he nodded at the bluff, "that. If I was gonna bushwhack somebody, that would sure be the place I'd choose."

Addie followed his eyes up and shrugged. "I don't see anything, Mr. Hooker."

"Don't mean nothin'."

She frowned. "I think you're being overly cautious, Mr. Hooker."

Jake shook his head. "Been a hunter too long not to know when game's turnin'."

"Can we go around?"

Jake nodded. "Could," he allowed. "But it would cost too much time if I'm wrong, or if he turns further on. 'Sides I can't take a chance on losin' those tracks. No, the only way is straight ahead." His eyes examined the bluff again. "Least I can do it my way," he said, and eased the horse out. "When I yell, hold on," he said.

"What are you going to do?"

"Haven't got time right now, just do what I tell you for once."

In the rocks on the bluff, Rem Sidy tried to get comfortable again, but there was a small spine of rock under him. It ran the length of his cover behind the boulder and was sharper than an unpaid whore's tongue.

"Damn," he swore.

"What?" Taylor asked from behind his rock, where he was sitting trying to get some rest.

"Nothin'," he snapped, and shook his head.

"Anything on the slope?"

"Hell, no," he answered, then glanced down. "If I—" His eyes jerked back. "Walt!" he whispered. "Walt—"

Canfield was next to him almost immediately.

Below them, the two people on the horse came up the slope slowly.

"How'd they get that far up?" he asked. "Fan," he motioned the men. "Let 'em come," he said. "Right up to the center of the clearing." Levering his rifle, he nosed it down-slope. And laying there waiting, he tried to make out the man's face, but he was too far away.

"Now?" Sidy whispered.

Canfield shook his head. "Not yet." He squinted, trying to get the man's face in focus. "A little more . . . just a lit-tle . . ."

Jake made himself ride slowly. If anybody was above them, they would be setting their aim, and that's what he wanted.

They neared the center of the clearing. Thirty feet or so.

The bluff was a hundred.

His eyes came back to the center of the clearing. And he yelled, screaming, kicking the horse out, bolting him forward, running out across the open ground.

For a half-second, he thought he had been wrong. Foolish.

Then the first shots came. Hitting wild. Two in front of them. Two more way downslope.

Kicking the roan, they lurched up the hill, driving for the bottom of the bluff.

Another flurry of shots kicked the dirt in front of them. The horse tried to shy, but Jake tore the reins around, kick-ing him again, pushing him up the slope and into the rocks.

Suddenly there was a wash of shots, mixing with their own sound, exploding down the slope.

"Addie," Jake screamed, and with one arm around her, he dove for the rocks, carrying them both down, and he could hear the lead tearing around them.

Twisting in the dirt, he looked back up at the horse and the rifle in the boot. He'd forgotten it.

"Dammit," he growled, starting for it.

The horse jerked around. Backpedaling down the slope, nearly falling trying to get away from the noise.

Jake reached for the reins, but the horse plummeted away from him, half-falling, half-running, down the slope and into the trees on the rim above the stream.

More shots smashed over the rocks.

"Crawl," Jake barked at Addie.

"Where?"

"Up there." Jake pointed into the rise of trees and boulders. "Now move."

Drawing the automatic, he raised up as Addie began scrambling, he emptied the gun into the rocks and followed her.

They pushed down through a narrow crevice, finding more cover, then down a fall, and stopped, Addie's breath clawing through her. Jake couldn't tell if it was fatigue or fear. Or both. All he knew was that it was both with him, but he didn't have time to think about it.

"Miss Ballard—" Jake turned to her. "You're about to get a rushed shooting lesson."

She stared the weapon. "I can't," she whispered. "I—"

"You're gonna have to," the old man growled. "Now, dammit, listen to me. To get out of here we're gonna have to do this together, or we're both gonna be dead. You hear me?"

She nodded stiffly. "I'll try."

"Try, hell, you'll do it."

He reloaded the empty automatic; then releasing the safety and sliding the action along its tracks, he cocked the hammer, rested it, and turning it in his hand, he held it out to the girl.

"Take it," he ordered her.

Addie's fingers touched, then closed around the handle and she stared at it, then looked up at the hunter.

"To fire it," he said, "you just pull the trigger. You've got seven shots. And they're gonna come hard. This thing kicks like hell, and the first time the noise is gonna scare the daylights out of you, and it'll feel like it's tryin' to break your arm. It won't. At least I don't think it will. Now don't try to aim. Just point it and squeeze. Remember that. Squeeze. And keep squeezing until it won't do nothin' no more," he swallowed. "You following all this—"

"Yes," she nodded, trying to seem suddenly confident. "I can do it."

Jake wiped sweat from his forehead. "I hope so," he sighed.

Canfield ran to the edge of the bluff and tried to pick the man and girl out of the boulders below. There were a few flickerings, then they were gone.

He looked back at Gage.

"You see his face?"

The big man shook his head. "No, but I did see the girl."

Canfield looked back down into the rocks. "Yeah," he nodded. "I did too. But the man—"

"I don't want to be killin' no girl," the big man growled.

Canfield's eyes snapped back. "Then let her stay out of the way. Otherwise it's her problem. And yours." He turned down the slope. "Now let's go."

Jake could hear them coming. Whisperings. Scrapings.

Looking back down the hill, he surveyed the naked slope. And shook his head.

No passage there.

Moving down and around a boulder, keeping low, he squinted into the sunlight up the slope along the access to the bluff.

A couple of more feet, he thought, and they would have made it. Been in the cover of the bluff and been able to flank them on the top.

But it was too late for that. He'd made a mistake, but one he had to make. Now he had to get himself out of it. And the girl.

Fifty or sixty feet away, he could see the bald finger of sandstone leading up, and on the other side, the scattering brush and pine. Then there was a drop to the rim above the stream bed.

Not much cover. Unless he could make it to that drop, then back down to the rim and the stream. Trouble was, he couldn't remember how steep that drop was.

And there wasn't any time to wonder.

Half-sounds nudged him, and taking Addie's arm, he pulled her up, angling along the rocks, keeping low, running for the spine leading upward, and the cover beyond.

They charged into a small clearing and two shots pounded the sandstone next to them. Hauling Addie, Jake plunged forward into the rocks on the other side, still running for the access.

Another shot exploded into the boulder behind them.

Pushing Addie down, Jake turned. Above him, he caught two flashes of color against the pale rocks.

He cocked the hammer, then holding the trigger back, he fanned the gun, not to hit anything, but to lay down fire.

The lead sprayed through the rocks, and Jake saw somebody diving for cover.

Motioning Addie, they ran again, with Jake leading. Coming down on the access, Jake pulled Addie to cover.

He pointed across the trail to the clearing and talked as he reloaded his gun.

"When I start shootin' again, you run like hell into that bunch of trees and brush there. Get way far down behind somethin' and when I yell you start shootin' up in there, and I'll come across. Like I said you won't hit anything. Just fire it. And stay low, somebody might shoot back."

Addie nodded, her eyes pale.

"You all right?" Jake asked.

"Yes," she forced her head to move. "I'm all right."

Jake's lips softened slightly, then the snap of gravel jerked his head around.

Tripping the hammer, he held the trigger back.

"Now," he shouted.

Addie stumbled to her feet, and pushing herself, ran, bolting into the open. Behind her, Jake lifted the pistol, fanning it again, sending lead pounding through the boulders.

His gun empty, Jake jerked back down, then turning saw Addie merge into the trees and brush.

A flurry of shots burst over him, pushing him down against

the sandstone. Looking across the trail again, he reloaded his gun.

The firing from above eased back, then quieted.

Cocking the pistol, Jake pulled his feet under him, and primed himself to run.

"Now," he shouted into the trees.

A breath's length passed and nothing happened.

"Addie," he barked.

Still nothing.

His eyes combed the area where he had seen the girl enter the brush.

There was no movement.

"Addie," he growled.

Sweat dripped salt into his eyes and he blinked it away, shoving his sleeve across his face. The heat seemed to thicken around him.

"Damn," he whispered, his hand tightening on the pistol and he trembled with a sudden loneliness. She had plenty of time. One of their shots must have . . .

A slug hit above him.

Then a second a few feet higher. Both were from the trees.

"Addie," he laughed, and jumped to his feet firing too, sending shots into the bluff along with those coming from across the trail.

Then reeling, he charged into the open.

Addie was still firing.

Two shots hit beside him, geysering sandstone into his eyes and chafing his face. The crash of gunfire roared around him, filling the sunlight. He felt a slug split the air beside him, another hit in front of him, and stumbling, diving, he plummeted into the cover of the pines.

More shots washed over him, exploding wood in a holocaust of splinters. Dragging his face out of the dust, his lungs cawing for air, he moved automatically, his legs and arms pulling, smashing through brush and small cactus without feeling the pain. He kept crawling.

A figure jerked in front of him and he pulled his gun up.

It was Addie.

"That way," he pointed down the hill. The more of the roll of the slope they could get between them and Canfield and his men the better cover they would have. Coming up behind her, he shoved on her buttocks. She looked back over her shoulder, nearly straightening up.

"Mr. Hooker . . ."

"Not now."

Jake pushed her again and they began to descend the slope. The ground began to fall away sharply, angling toward the drop above the stream bed.

A shot hammered the ground behind them, then a tree trunk beside them. Pushing Addie on, Jake reeled, firing.

A figure plunged from the rocks, charging into the open, pumping rifle fire toward Jake.

The lead raked the branches above him, and hitting the ground, Jake placed a careful shot at the running figure, doubling him, piling him into the dirt.

The man in the dirt screamed. "Walt," he yelled, his voice ragged. "I'm hit."

An old man, Jake saw. About his age. Holding his leg.

He had a clear shot. He could finish him.

The old man screamed again. Helpless.

Frowning, Jake shook his head. He couldn't kill a man like that. Hauling his gun around, he took Addie's arm and pressed down the hill, rushing through the trees until the ground flattened slightly. Then there was nothing. Only a crest.

"Damn," he growled.

Below them the bank fell away nearly straight off into the stream a hundred feet below.

Kneeling, Jake examined the bank. The walls were dirt and gravel mostly, with some rock outcroppings and a few knots of brush and pine.

"Mr. Hooker," Addie said, "I don't think we can get down there—"

"We're gonna have to," Jake said, and began reloading his gun.

"Mr. Hooker," she protested.

"Dammit," Jake snapped, finishing with his gun and jamming it in his belt. "There's no time for a vote," he said and took the automatic from her. He loaded it quickly, then slipped it in its holster.

"Now let's get goin'—" he ordered her and grasping her hand, they started over the side.

Canfield squeezed through the rocks and down to the bottom of the bluff. Kneeling behind a small piñon pine, he could see Sidy sprawled in the open. Not moving, but still breathing. The only blood Canfield could see on him was his leg.

He raised his eyes from Sidy to the trees. Nothing.

Behind him, Taylor and Gage scraped through the rocks and down beside him.

"Stay down," he snapped. "We're—"

"Rem," Taylor whispered, seeing the old man. "Sonofabitch shot Rem."

"Howie," Canfield began.

"He shot Rem," the boy raged, bolting to his feet.

Canfield reached for him, but he was already running, charging into the open, his rifle in front of him.

"Howie," Gage screamed.

The boy rushed by Sidy, and pumping his rifle, he plunged into the trees, and was gone.

Then silence.

Canfield waited for return gunfire, but there was none.

"Rem," he said to Gage, "you take the left."

Nodding, Gage turned, then they were both on their feet running, pulling for the old man. Gage rushed in on his left, Canfield on the right, both men grasping the old man's armpits, jerking him upright, then hauling him toward the trees.

Sidy screamed, fighting them, but they kept running, tearing into the trees, and down the slope to cover.

They dropped him and Sidy barked, then moaned, pushing his face into the dirt and pine needles. "Jesus," he whispered. "Oh sweet Christ . . ."

Canfield glanced at the leg.

"Stop prayin', Rem," he said. "You ain't gonna die. Not too quick anyway."

The old man's only reply was another moan.

Canfield's eyes swept the trees. Still nothing.

"Where you figger?" Gage asked him.

Canfield shook his head. "Down," he guessed. "Maybe back toward the falls. Let's move that way." He put his hand out to Gage. "And move carefully," he said.

Jake and the girl eased down the slope slowly. Jake first, Addie following. Walking sideways, he was able to get footing in the loose dirt.

"Stay close," Jake said.

"Stop ordering me—"

"You're picking a hellava time for a discussion, Miss Ballard."

They moved down and Jake held onto a small bush, easing his foot down again, making for a scattering of small pines about twenty feet away.

Stepping again, his boot scraped over a vein of rock and he slipped down, slamming to one knee, and caught the branches of a stickleaf, his hand crushing the yellow flowers.

"Lucky that time." He swallowed with difficulty. "Watch the rock," he said to Addie. "It's bad footing."

Pushing himself up, he moved again, cautiously making his way toward the trees.

They came down into an outcropping of rock, through it, then down another ten feet, and through the branches of the pines.

Kneeling down, Jake eased his breath through him. Ad-

die sat down behind a tree and pulled off her hat. It was
cool under the pines and a rustling of wind touched them.

Jake slumped against the trunk of a tree and wiped the
sweat from his face. Looking down, he noticed the cactus
needles in his leg for the first time.

"Christ," he grumbled, and jerked one from his pant,
and sighed.

"Are you hurt, Mr. Hooker?"

"No, ma'am. Just cactus needles."

"Can I help?"

"No, thank you, miss. It'll have to wait a bit. We get a
little further down this slope and we'll have enough cover
to be clear of 'em for a while."

Standing, he edged down from the trees. He had just
stepped away from the pines when a shot ripped through
the bark of the tree beside him. Then another.

Jake lunged back, landing on his shoulder and rolling,
shots exploding the dirt around him, until he was behind
the tree again.

"Stay down," he shouted to Addie.

A rifle crashed up the slope, blowing lead through the
branches around them.

Slipping his pistol from its leather, Jake chanced a look
up the bank. A slug blasted the wood above his head.

"Just one," he said, swearing softly. "Can't get a shot at
him. He can keep us here until the others come if we don't
get him."

The hunter looked back to the outcropping of rock, then
up the slope.

"I've gotta try and get over there," he said, pointing to
the rocks. "I can get a clear shot from there."

Addie stared at him a moment.

"Mr. Hooker . . ."

Jake saw the concern in her eyes and tried to smile, but
didn't make it.

"Stay down," he growled, and looked back up toward the
rocks.

Bringing the automatic up, he fired twice, then was on his feet, running, firing again, and diving for the cover of the outcropping.

A shot ripped above him and he pulled his head out of the dirt.

Another shot blasted a spray of rock over him.

He let a third go over, then bolted upright pumping lead up the slope.

From behind a rock someone screamed, then stumbled to the edge, levering his rifle, firing as he fell.

The slug hit in front of Jake, exploding rock into his face; reeling, staggering backward, Jake lost his footing, and he was falling, crashing down the slope, slamming through dirt and stone, ripping through branches. He heard someone scream. Addie. He flailed to catch himself, but his hands were torn open, pounded, then something rammed into his arm, bending it, and he heard it snap. Screaming, he hit bottom. And sudden darkness.

As the first shots crashed, Canfield was just above the falls. Gage, a little below him on the rim.

Canfield reeled, waiting.

Another shot echoed. And another.

"Up the slope," Gage shouted.

"Damn," Canfield swore, bolting out. "I guessed wrong," he breathed, running harder, hearing more shots. "I guessed wrong."

Sobbing, Addie rushed from the trees, then sinking to her knees, looked at where Jake had fallen. For a moment, she couldn't believe it. He still seemed to be hovering in the air. Falling.

Then she saw him. Lying on his stomach. His left arm twisted up behind him horribly.

And he moved. Jerking slightly. Then he was still again.

"Mr. Hooker," she whispered, and standing, she ran back to the trees where the slope was easier and started down.

She crawled. Moving slowly. Wanting to run. Scraping through the dirt. Finally reaching the bottom. She ran to him, kneeling at his side.

"Mr. Hooker," she said, and touched him.

A moan whispered from him and he stirred slightly, then slumping down, was motionless again.

Addie touched his face, then lifted it. He was breathing. Reaching down to turn him over, she brushed his twisted arm. A spasm hammered through him, and he screamed like a child crying.

"Mr. Hooker," she said, brushing the dirt and hair from his face. "Mr. Hooker?"

His cry eased into labored breathing and he was quiet. Half-conscious.

Above her, she heard the sound of running and branches breaking.

"Mr. Hooker." She shook his head. "Please—"

The running sound was coming closer.

Her eyes came back down and moved frantically over the stream bank. She had to get him out of sight. There was no cover on this side. Across the stream and down was a stand of trees.

Coming around by his head, Addie reached down and grasped Jake under the armpits. He cried out again, but she lifted him up anyway, hauling around to the stream, and backing into it, she dragged him.

The rushing water hit her hard, its cold shocking her. She lost her footing, plunging down into the water, and bolted up again.

Above her, gravel began to rattle down the slope, and looking up, she could see two figures on the rim.

The water took a little of the unconscious man's weight away, but he was still heavy, and she pulled, wondering how long she could keep it up.

On the slope, she saw the flicker of color, and a quick glimpse of the figures running through the trees.

The stream deepened under Addie, coming up around

her waist, the current strengthening, carrying her back. Fighting the water, and still hauling Jake, her foot slipped, and she dropped completely under, pulling him down with her.

Bursting back to the top, Addie hauled Jake with her. The cold water revived him slightly and his left arm lashed out wildly. He shoved against her weakly, but she was able to keep a tight grip around his shoulder. He struggled against her, then slumped down, unconscious again.

Addie stumbled on the shale of the opposite shore, the water dropping away as they started up. Jake was like lead again. Her legs and arms strained dragging him. Slowly. Out of the water. Into the grass, and finally the trees.

Charging around an outcropping, through some brush, Canfield saw the body on the crest and stopped, holding his hand out to Gage.

He brought his gun up, cocking it, and stepped forward slowly.

The man on the ground was Taylor.

Crouching, slipping through the trees, he and Gage made their way to him. Keeping low, he reached out and turned the boy over.

He was still alive. But that was all. His shirt front was soaked with blood.

"Got 'im, boss," the boy coughed, his mouth working mechanically against a red paste. "I got 'im—"

"Where?" Canfield asked.

"Below." Taylor forced the words. "Fell."

Canfield and Gage eased to the rim.

"You see anything?" he asked Gage after a moment.

Frowning, the big man shook his head.

Canfield looked back to Taylor.

"You sure, boy? You sure you got him?"

The boy nodded jerkily. "Know I did," he whispered. "Know—"

Canfield touched his shoulder. "All right," he said gently, "Just take it easy. You're gonna be fine," he lied.

"Sure I got him," Taylor insisted.

Canfield nodded. "Yeah, most likely you did," he assured him quietly. "You did a good job."

The boy blinked. "Did . . ."

Canfield smiled. "You were the best of the bunch," he said.

A tremor touched the boy's mouth. "Was . . ." He swallowed. "Boss, I—" He reached up for Canfield but didn't make it. He sighed slightly, then was staring at Canfield. And past him.

Canfield pressed his eyes closed. "Damn," he whispered, and opened them again, his hand tightening on his gun.

He stood up.

"Let's go find him," he said to Gage. "You take the far side, I'll—"

"Wait," Gage interrupted him, "We ain't got the time. We're gonna be gettin' to Long's Meadow after Ballard as is—"

"He'll wait," Canfield said. "That fella—"

"That fella's most likely dead. Taylor said he got him."

"Then where is he?"

Gage shrugged. "In the stream, maybe. Walt, like you always say, we got a job to do."

Canfield looked at him and blinked. "Yeah," he admitted, "you're right."

"The guns are the important thing. Not him."

"Yeah," Canfield nodded, staring back down the slope, a tightness gathering in his chest. "Just wonder what—"

"Don't matter," Gage said. "Come on."

"No," he said, not believing it, then turned back up the slope. "Let's get Rem and get the hell out of here."

# EIGHTEEN

Addie watched the men turn away from the crest. Lying painfully still on the ground next to Jake, she waited another minute, then shuddering, breathed again.

Pushing herself up, she turned to Jake and touched his face.

He stirred slightly.

Trembling, she shook him gently, whispering, "Mr. Hooker?"

His eyes fluttered open and he looked at her. "Miss Ballard . . ." he muttered, and his eyes widened. "The others," he remembered, jerking upright, and screamed as the pain from his arm jolted him back.

Addie quickly pushed her hand to his mouth and eased him back.

Swallowing, he pressed the pain back, nodding to her, and she took her hand away.

Trembling, he looked at the arm. "Busted?" he asked.

She nodded. "I think so."

His eyes came up, skimming through the trees. "Canfield . . . ?"

"I don't know." She shook her head. "We have to move. Can you walk?"

He frowned, wagging his shaggy head. "Don't figger I can. Not on my own steam." He reached out to her. "Help me up."

Taking his arm, she lifted him around and up. His legs were weak, trembling, and putting his weight on them, he sank back to the ground. Wordlessly, she knelt down, and dragging him, she pulled him up again, taking more of his weight on her. "Let's go," she ordered him.

His feet scraped forward, and they moved, stumbling heavily through the brush and limbs up an easy rise and over it.

Coming down the other side, Addie staggered under his weight, regained her feet, then stepped through a rotten log; her knees collapsed, sending them both crashing through the brush with Jake landing on top of her.

More tired than hurt, Addie lay slumped quiet, trying to gather her strength.

"Damn," Jake whispered above her, and she could hear the pain in his voice.

"Your arm?" she asked.

He nodded stiffly. "Be all right."

Struggling, she pushed him off her, and sat up next to him.

Jake was trembling. There was sweat mixed with the water on his face. He shook his head. "No good," he whispered. "I—"

Above them, on the other side of the hill, leaves were crushed. Footfalls.

Jake's eyes snapped to Addie and he motioned her down; then rolling onto his back, he lifted himself on his good elbow and propped his back against the trunk of a tree. He reached down for the automatic. The holster was empty. And looking down, he remembered he had been using it on the slope. It was probably still there someplace.

The footfalls came again. Heavy. Slow.

Fumbling, he grasped the single-action in his belt, and tugged it free.

The gun was incredibly heavy. His thumb slipped on the hammer several times, and shaking his head, he looked at Addie.

She was watching him.

"Up to you," he said, and handed it to her. "Cock the hammer," he said, "and pull the trigger."

She clicked the hammer back prone. Waiting.

"Wait'll you can see somethin'," he whispered. Then added, "Maybe we'll get lucky."

The footfalls were nearing the top. Pushing through branches.

Whoever it was, Jake thought, they ain't comin' careful.

On the hill, the footfalls topped the crest.

"Ready," Jake said.

Movement. A shadow.

Addie raised the gun. Holding it with both hands.

Jake could see the beginnings of form now coming over the top—

Addie's finger tightened on the trigger.

A little more of the figure showed.

Addie's mouth set, her muscles drawing tight—and Jake whisper-shouted suddenly.

"No," he barked, laughing. "No—it's the roan."

He pushed the gun down as the horse came over the hill, grazing as he walked, searching for better grass.

"Damn . . ." Jake smiled. "I think we just got lucky."

Addie coughed suddenly and began crying and laughing at the same time.

"It's all right," Jake assured her. "It's all right. Come on," he said, taking the gun back and putting it in the holster, slipping the thong on the hammer. "Catch up that animal and let's make tracks."

After getting Jake up on the horse, Addie led him out, threading her way through the hills.

In the saddle, Jake felt every movement of the horse in his arm like hammer blows. Leaning forward, keeping most of his weight on the opposite leg helped some, but not much.

He waited until they were well away from the creek, then looked for cover. They had just come around a small hill when he spotted a stand of rocks.

"There," he called to Addie, gesturing with his head.

The girl took them in, then helped Jake down.

He slumped back against a small boulder, his breath aching in him, sweat thick on his back, chest, and face.

"Let me see to that arm," Addie said.

Jake shook his head. "No," he swallowed. "Best rest a bit—"

"Mr. Hooker," Addie frowned. "I don't need rest as much as we need to look at that arm."

"Yes,'m," he nodded. "You do. You're gonna need it bad. 'Cause in a while, you're gonna have a hellava job to do—"

# NINETEEN

Looking back, Walt Canfield watched the darkness come.

Sitting hunkered down, leaning against a pine, he held a cup of coffee cradled in his hand and felt the black chill drift over him, and between him and the others. Sidy on his blankets, asleep, head propped up on the underside of his saddle. Gage tending the fire, sipping coffee. The twilight negated them into form only, dark movements. Echoes.

Shivering slightly, Canfield stood up and walked back to the fire, and kneeling down beside Gage, he poured himself another cup of coffee.

He let his eyes wander to Sidy.

"How he doin'?" he asked Gage.

The thick-shouldered man shrugged. "Stopped bleedin' and the bullet went through. But he's gonna slow us."

"Yeah," Canfield frowned. "We'll take him into Miller's Store and leave him."

"Be best," Gage agreed.

Canfield's gaze lingered on the old man for a moment. "Dammit . . ." he whispered.

Gage's eyes narrowed. "Thought you didn't like him."

Canfield's eyes stayed on the old man. "I . . . don't," he replied quietly, watching Sidy as if he were a reflection; then blinking, Canfield stood up. "I don't," he said again. "Just don't like losin' men." He turned his gaze down the slope. "That's three now. Three to that sonofabitch, whoever he is."

Gage looked up. "You figger he's still alive?"

Canfield shook his head. "I don't know. That's the problem. I just goddamn don't know. He ain't predictable. If

I knew what he wanted. Why? I'd know what to do about him. But I don't. He's like a damn—" He shrugged the word away.

"Ghost." Gage said it for him.

Canfield's eyes jerked to him, then he forced a smile through his tight lips. "Yeah," he nodded. "If I believed in 'em."

Gage poured himself another cup of coffee, his eyes holding Canfield. "First time I ever knew you to let personals enter into a job."

Canfield's gaze hardened. "The job'll get done," he assured Gage tersely, then let his eyes slip back to the darkness. "You know," he said after a moment, "I almost hope he ain't dead," the ex-soldier whispered. "I want to know what's keepin' him comin'. What makes him run. Once I know that, I'll have the edge on him . . . and I'll take him."

"Just like that."

"Yeah," Canfield nodded, his trembling hand tightening on his coffee cup. "Just like that."

# TWENTY

Leaning with his back to a rock, Jake looked at Addie curled up on the ground. She had fallen asleep where she had sat down.

He raised his hand and pushed at the thick sweat chilling on his face. The movement tugged at his broken arm, and easing his hand back down, he closed his eyes and frowned.

He couldn't wait any longer. It had to be done now.

Opening his eyes, he leaned forward and touched the girl gently.

She jerked awake; then blinking, she remembered where she was and sat up.

"Are we moving again?" she asked sleepily. Nearly child-like.

Jake felt the impulse to smile, then lost it. He shook his head. "No," he swallowed. "We ain't movin'. I'm afraid you've got a job of work to do."

Her eyes went to his arm, and she trembled. "I don't know if I can."

"You can," he nodded.

"How do you know?"

"Because you have to."

A frown pressed her mouth. "Sometimes you're terribly optimistic."

"Comes in handy."

Her eyes came up, the frown whispering into a smile. "You're also a stubborn sonofabitch."

"That's been said before," he nodded, and looked down at the arm. "You're gonna have to do it," he said. "If it ain't done, it'll heal like that, then have to be busted again. And that don't exactly appeal to me."

She nodded reluctantly, surrendering. "All right," she said. "What—"

"Coat comes off first," he said.

Taking a breath, Addie started. Pulling him forward. Slipping the coat off the good arm. Then around. Easing it down the broken one.

She could feel Jake shiver as she tugged the sleeve. She looked up at him.

"Keep goin'," he hissed, the pain tautening his jaw and throat, cording down into his chest.

Her eyes went back to the sleeve. She grasped it tighter. Tugging slowly, easing it down and off.

Jake sat back against the rock, his breath fluttering.

"Mr. Hooker . . ."

"All right," he managed to nod. "Doin' fine. Have you skinnin' beaver in no time." He tried to smile, then he sat forward holding the arm out.

Addie looked at it. Beneath the covering of the sleeve she could tell it was swollen badly halfway between his elbow and wrist.

"Best tear the shirt," he said. "Don't know if we could get it off that or not."

Nodding, Addie unbuttoned the shirt cuff, and pulling easily and steady, she began to tear it.

Watching her, Jake laughed suddenly. Stopping, Addie looked up questioningly.

Jake shook his head. "This here's supposed to be the finest shirt in the store where I bought it," he sighed, "and it tears like a spiderweb. Sometimes I'm grateful for the modern age."

"Mr. Hooker—"

He looked down. "What?"

"Shut up."

Still smiling, trembling, he nodded. "Go to it," he said.

Addie looked to the sleeve. Straining at the material. It

tore easily, but as it went over the wound, as flimsy as it was, she could feel Jake tremble.

"There," she said.

Jake nodded, his body still stiff, trying to relax.

"Now the work," he breathed.

Addie nodded. "All right," she said, and reaching out, touched his arm.

A spasm bolted through him. "Doin' fine," he said raggedly, his breath coming hard. "Now feel for the break."

Addie's hands moved again, and Jake trembled.

"Here," she said finally.

Jake nodded. "Most likely I'm gonna pass out in a second, so let me finish. Grab the arm just above the break with one hand, and my hand with the other. Then pull. Straight. The bone should slide back in place, but you'll be able to know now by feelin'."

Addie looked up at his face. A smile twitched on his mouth, and there was a gentleness in his eyes for her.

"Mr. Hooker . . ."

"Best thing to do is let me have it all at once. Not let me know when it's comin'. Muscle'll be relaxed—least a bit. Think about all the times you been mad—all the times you wanted to hurt somebody, hell, I know there's been many a time—"

And she jerked, wrenching up and pulling out, snapping the arm straight.

She had expected him to scream, but he didn't. His body bolted upright, his eyes widening. Then he quivered slightly. There was a catch in his voice and she could almost feel the pain exploding through him.

His body shook, the sound of his breathing tearing through him like something raw.

"Splint it," he growled tightly, and swallowed, still trembling. "Use a drink . . ." he whispered, his gaze slipping to Addie slowly. "Sure could . . ." Then his eyes blanked, his body drifting limp, and he passed out in her arms.

Holding him, she trembled too. "So could I, Mr. Hooker . . . so could I . . ."

After splinting the arm, Addie got up to get the water from the horse.

"Dyin' . . . Jake murmured.

Addie looked back around.

Still asleep, Jake stirred, trying to move, muttering fragments of words.

Addie knelt beside him. "Mr. Hooker," she whispered, and touched him. His hand shot out, grasping her arm, holding it tight. She put her hand on his to push it away and she could feel him trembling.

"It's all dyin' . . ." he choked, his voice grating, fragile.

"Mr. Hooker," she said, and tried to pull away, but he held her tighter.

"Killed you, Pa. Angie, get up. Get up. Ma. Ethan . . . Bastards'll kill ever'thin' . . . don't belong . . . don't belong . . ."

"You're all right, Mr. Hooker," Addie assured him. "You're all right."

"Cold," he shivered. "Coldest winter I ever seen. Don't belong, I—"

Addie touched his face. It was wet. Reaching down, she pulled the blanket up over both of them, and her eyes went to his face again.

He was quieter now, but his hand still held her tight.

She tried to ease away, but his hand gripped her harder, and sitting there, she stared down at him for a long time, a strange rustling aching through her. Something she had never felt before.

Being needed.

# TWENTY-ONE

The smell of coffee awakened him.

Rustling in the blankets, Jake had trouble moving his left arm. It was heavy. Dead. Looking down, he saw the splint on it, and remembered it was broken.

He frowned slightly, then smelled the coffee again. A beginning of saliva wet his mouth.

Addie was in front of him, tending the fire. The frown began to give way to a half-smile. Nice, he thought—then realized—

"Damn," he barked, and jerking the blanket off he bolted up, carrying it with him, pushing Addie aside, and throwing the blanket over the fire, smothering it.

"What in the world?" Addie blurted.

"Smoke," Jake said, stamping the fire. "They might see it."

Addie scrambled to her feet.

"Do you know how long it took me to make that fire?" she exploded.

"Miss—"

"I went to a damned lot of trouble to make us some coffee, and now you've probably spilled it all over the place."

"Those men—"

"I know it," she raged. "I know it. I just thought you might . . ." She caught herself and stammered. "I mean, it might do you some good."

"Oh," Jake frowned, embarrassed. "Well, I—" he began, and ran out of words.

Avoiding his eyes, Addie knelt beside the remains of the

fire, and reaching under the blanket, she smiled. Lifting
the blanket back, she pulled out the pot. It was upright.

"Looks like you're not as much of an oaf as you try to
be," she smiled.

Jake finished his coffee, and pouring another cup, glanced
at the girl. There was something about her this morning.
Every time she looked at him, he felt clumsy.

Her eyes came up and he smiled suddenly.

"The coffee," he nodded; "almost worth all the trouble."

"Almost," she allowed.

Draining the cup, he handed it to her and pushed himself
up with his good hand.

"Best get goin'," he sighed, looking into the coming
morning.

"Can you ride all right?" Addie asked.

"I'll have to," he said.

Nodding, Addie picked up the cups and emptied the pot,
then with Jake clumsily helping, she began to saddle the
horse.

"Let me do this," she said.

Shrugging, Jake stood back reluctantly. "Just don't do it
wrong."

"Why don't you let me do it, then we'll see if it's wrong."

"Women," Jake grumbled, standing back. He watched
as she finished with the saddle, and then he frowned.

She did it right.

Turning, she grinned at him victoriously.

"Well?"

"You been payin' attention."

"There's not much else to do."

"Cinch could be tighter," he pointed out. "He'll suck up
that bloat later."

"I'll tighten it later," she said, and smiled. "You don't
give an inch do you?"

"With you I've learned not to."

"You're not exactly the most amiable person I know of either," she countered.

"Miss Ballard—"

"Yes, Mr. Hooker?" She was smiling again.

"I—" he started, then sighed it away. "All right, goddammit, will you help me up so we can get out of here."

"My pleasure."

Jake grasped the saddle horn, and with Addie pushing on his rear, he bellied into the leather and sat up.

"Damn," he whispered, swallowing, the sweat starting already; nausea flushed over him, but he held himself in the saddle.

"Mr. Hooker—"

"All right," he growled. He didn't look at her. He could already feel the concern in her voice. He didn't want to see it in her eyes. "Time we were at it."

She followed him up.

"Mr. Hooker, perhaps, you—"

"I'm doin' fine, dammit, will you just let me be?"

"Well, I'm just tryin' to help," she snapped. "There's no need to be so damned obstinate."

"What—?"

"Bullheaded."

"Oh," he nodded.

They started up a small hill, and he glanced back at her.

"Ah, Miss Ballard . . ."

"Yes."

"You"—he cleared his throat—"you done a good job yesterday. On my arm. Gettin' me across the creek. All the way around. I . . . ahh . . ."

"What?"

"Thanks," he mumbled, giving up the words as if they were being pulled from him.

Her eyes darkened. "You're welcome, Mr. Hooker," she acknowledged quietly.

Jake looked at her. "Something wrong?"

She shook her head. "No," she whispered, and dropped her eyes, avoiding his gaze.

Jake continued to stare at her for a moment, then turned in the saddle, feeling suddenly angry without knowing why.

"Women," he grumbled.

# TWENTY-TWO

The sun was approaching eleven when Canfield topped the small rise. Below him, a mile away, he could see the scrawl of corrals and the smudge of Miller's Store against the green of the valley floor.

He looked back at Gage and Sidy following him. Gage was leading Sidy's horse and the old man was leaning heavily in the saddle.

"Miller's," he called to them.

Sidy's head bobbed up. His face looked like it was made of wax and dust.

"Get somebody to look at that leg," Canfield said. "Pour a couple of drinks down you to boot."

Sidy managed a pale smile.

Canfield was turning back around when he saw the wetness on Sidy's leg.

He was bleeding again.

"Nothin'," the old man grinned weakly. "Hell, you get a bandage on me, and a drink in me, I'll be good as new."

"Sure you will," Canfield said, and quickly turned his horse out, kicking him over the rise and down toward the store.

The longer Jake was in the saddle, the more the rhythm of the horse began to grind into his arm. He tried to concentrate on the tracks he was following, but the pain was always there, like a hammer.

Coming up a small hill, he almost missed the leavings of the campsite. He was on top of the remains of the fire when he saw it.

"Damn," he frowned, and dismounting clumsily, he knelt beside the fire, holding his hand down to the coals.

"Four hours," he said to himself, and standing again, he saw the drops of blood on the ground.

He nodded.

"The one I hit's still alive," he said. "That'll slow 'em. Means we gotta make time."

"Mr. Hooker," Addie protested. "Your arm—"

"My arm's fine," he snapped, and walking back to the horse, he grasped the horn and pulled himself up awkwardly.

"I could have helped you," Addie said as he butted the saddle.

"Didn't need it," he lied without looking at her, and turned the horse out, starting up the hills.

The slope of the land steepened and Jake found he was having to keep himself in the saddle by holding the horn. The sun began to swim above him and a gradual sweat matted his shirt and face.

His hand tightened on the saddle horn.

"Mr. Hooker," Addie said behind him.

"Yes, ma'am?"

"Are you all right?"

Jake smiled thinly. "Just a little warm," he swallowed.

The horse sidestepped under them and Jake's breath caught as the pain spiked through him. It even seemed to be in his eyes and teeth.

"Maybe a little water would help," Addie offered.

Jake glanced down at the canteen. "Yeah," he agreed. "It might at that."

With the horse still moving, Jake let go of the horn and slipped the canteen free. The sudden weight in his hand and the movement of the horse pulled him sideways, and he felt himself tipping out of the saddle.

He dropped the canteen and would have followed, but Addie's arms pushed around him, giving him balance.

Sitting upright, he was able to stop the horse; then wrapping the reins around the horn, he leaned forward, shaking his head.

"Dizzy," he said. "Just a might whirly in my head."

Addie dismounted, then helped him down. As he stepped down from the stirrups, his knees gave under him and he sat down in the dust.

"Don't move," Addie ordered him, and walking back down the hill, she picked up the canteen and brought it to him. Uncapping it, she poured some into her hand, wiping his face with it, then tipped it to his mouth for him to drink.

Nodding, he pushed it away.

"That'll do," he said.

Addie drank; then capping it again, she stood and hung it back on the saddle horn.

"I'll take the reins," she said.

Jake looked up, then managed to stand. "You'll what—?"

"I'm taking the reins," Addie repeated determinedly.

"Look," Jake started.

Addie cut him off. "You're in no condition. You'll pass out before long. Riding behind, maybe you can sleep. At least you'll still be going."

Jake stared at her. He started to say something, but sighed instead. Unfortunately, she was right.

She helped him up, and he moved back. She came up into the saddle and unwound the reins.

"Hup," she said to the horse, and they began to move.

Behind her, Jake shook his head.

"Shows me how much the world's changin'," he grumbled disgustedly. "Ridin' behind a woman."

Reining up in front of the store, Canfield and Gage lowered Sidy out of the saddle, and each man taking one arm, they walked him across the small porch and through the door.

The store was a huge one-room morass of tables, shelves, and counters, littered with canned goods, clothing, and hardware.

A round-bellied, bald-headed man looked up from behind a long slab of wood propped up on barrels to the
right of the three men as they came in the door. He was
leaning on the slab, drinking a beer. His eyes went to the
blood on Sidy's leg, and setting the beer down, he straightened up.

"You fellas got trouble?" he asked.

"A little," Canfield nodded. "You Miller?"

"So my mother claimed."

"We could use a room if you got it, and somebody
that knows somethin' about doctorin'."

Miller came around the counter, pointing the way through
the cluttered store. "Room's out back here. Ain't much but
a bed—"

"It'll do," Canfield said as he and Gage followed, carrying
Sidy.

"No doctor though. Wife knows some about carin'."

They went through a door and along a wooden walk in
front of a low building built onto the store. Miller shoved
the first door open and pointed the way inside.

Canfield and Gage walked Sidy into the room and sat him
down on the narrow bed.

Canfield looked up and around. The room was small and
dark. Dirt floor. It was dank with the smell of wanderers and
time. He felt a brush of something, as if something dark had
passed, and swallowing, he looked to Sidy.

"How you doin'?"

"All right," the old man nodded; then his eyes came up.
"How 'bout some whiskey for the pain?"

Canfield looked to Miller standing in the door, peering
in curiously. "Bring it to him. Maybe your wife could see to
him pretty quick. We're in kind of a hurry."

"Hurry," grumbled Miller, turning out the door. "Ever'-
body's in a hurry. Fella early this mornin' didn't even stop
ten minutes—"

Canfield followed him. "You say another fella was
through?"

The storekeeper stopped and looked back at him. "That's right," he nodded. "Asked the way to Long's Meadow."

"In his fifties? Well dressed?"

"That's him."

"Say his name by any chance?"

"Ballard."

"Anybody with him?"

Miller shook his head. "Nope." His eyes narrowed questioningly. "You know him?"

"Yeah," Canfield smiled. "I know him." He glanced back at Gage. "Phil," he said, "let's get us a meal and a round of drinks. Somethin's finally goin' right."

Miller served them their meal at the bar. They were finishing when the door to the back slammed. Canfield's eyes came up. Mrs. Miller came into the store. She was large and round-bellied, too, a near twin of her husband except that she wasn't bald.

"Your friend's lost a lot of blood," she said, wiping her hands on her dress and coming around behind the bar with her husband. She poured herself a drink. "Be all right in a week or so." She downed the drink and poured herself another.

"Figured that," Canfield frowned. "Can he stay here?"

"That's what the room is for," Miller answered.

Nodding, Canfield put his glass out. Mrs. Miller poured him one and he downed it.

"Best be movin'," he said to Gage.

"Who's gonna tell Rem?"

Canfield frowned. "I will," he said. "You get the supplies."

Reaching behind the bar, he slipped two bottles down, and carrying them, walked out the back door.

He strode down the walk to the small door and went in. Sidy was sitting on his bed, a bottle in his hand.

"Brought you some fresh goods," Canfield said, coming into the room, tossing the bottles on the bed.

Sidy grinned, his old face red with whiskey. "Ain't seen this much coffin varnish in a long time. Have one—"

Canfield glanced around the room. Taking the wad of bills Taylor had taken off the dead man at the stage stop from his pocket, he peeled off a fifty and put it on the bed. The closeness of the room seemed to press in on him.

"Payday," Sidy grinned.

"Gage and I are leavin'," Canfield told him. "The money's for you."

The old man stared up at him uncomprehending. "What—?"

Canfield avoided his eyes. "We gotta move fast, you know that. You'll slow us down. Stay here a couple of weeks, then catch up with us in Sonora. 'Sides, all that whiskey," he forced himself to smile, "you can have a hellava time."

Sidy blinked, then his face parted in a grin. "Yeah, that ain't bad at all. See you fellas down in Sonora." He waved at the bottles. "Have a drink."

"No." Canfield shook his head, his eyes moving restlessly over the room again, and the man on the bed, faceless in its darkness.

"See you," Canfield said, turning and rushing out, pulling the door shut behind him.

Ten minutes later he and Gage were in the saddle pulling up the slopes, but he could still feel the small room around him and the old man sitting lost in it.

# TWENTY-THREE

Addie reined in on the crest above Miller's Store.

"Mr. Hooker," she said.

Behind her, Jake had already seen it. "Miller's," he nodded, squinting into the late afternoon sunlight.

"Don't see 'em," he frowned.

"Their horses could be in the corral," Addie pointed out.

Jake glanced at her and smiled faintly. "Could be," he acknowledged; then his eyes moved back to the store and the smile faded. "Ain't nothin' to do but go down."

Addie looked back at him. "But your arm, are you—"

"Doin' better," Jake nodded. "Ridin' behind I been able to cushion it with my good hand. Good idea you had," he allowed grudgingly, then gestured toward Miller's with his head. "We ain't gonna get nowhere sitting here."

Frowning, Addie turned front in the saddle and eased the horse out. They came down off the hill slowly. To the base and out across the flat. A hundred and fifty yards from the store, Jake reached forward, touching the reins.

"Draw him in," he said, and Addie did.

As the horse stepped to a halt, Jake slipped off the back.

"I'll walk in," he said. "With this arm, I'll have a better chance on the ground if anything starts." He pointed off toward the corrals. "You head that way if there's any shooting."

He looked back to the store, and taking his Colt from its holster, he started walking.

He was twenty yards from the building when the door opened. Jake was bringing the gun up when he recognized

Miller's stomach coming through the door, his arms full of flour sacks.

Jake lowered the gun as Miller eased the sacks to the porch.

Straightening, he saw the girl, then Jake, his broken arm, and the gun in his hand.

"Rough day, Jake?" Miller called.

"Fairly," the old hunter nodded, and walked in. "You seen anything of three fellas, one of 'em hit?"

"Trouble?"

Jake's eyes narrowed. "Ain't got time for a social, Ed. They been here or not?"

A nervous smile ticked the storekeeper's lips, and he nodded. "Matter of fact, one of 'em's still here."

Jake cocked the gun in his hand.

"Where is he?"

"Room out back—"

"And your missus?"

"Feedin' the stock."

"Get her," Jake said, and nodded toward Addie. "And take her with you. Keep 'em both down."

"Listen, Jake, is there—"

"Do it," Jake ordered him. "Quick."

Rem Sidy stretched in his bed, and reaching for another bottle, he knocked it over the edge, smashing it on the floor.

"Damn," he burped, and looked around the bed for another. There was none. "Damn," he sighed again, and looked up. "Hey," he shouted. No answer. He shouted again. Again no answer. "Haveta do it myself," he slurred. "Get my ass half shot off and gotta get up and get my own whiskey. Not fair."

Pushing his hands down on the bed, he lifted himself up weavingly, and stood. The whiskey had deadened some of the pain in the leg, and he found, by putting very little weight on it, he could walk.

"Better already," he mused, and grinned.

Hopping to the door, he opened it; then using the wall for support, he stumbled down the walk and into the store. The bar and whiskey behind it were right in front of him.

He grinned again. For once things were going right for him.

He hopped to the bar, and around it, looking over the whiskey on the wall.

Unable to make up his mind, he rested back against the bar for a moment; then shrugging and reaching up, he heard the door slam behind him. With the bottle in his hand, he turned.

"Hey, Miller," he said.

But it wasn't Miller. It was somebody else. And there was a gun in his hand.

Dropping the bottle, shattering it on the floor, he fumbled for his own gun.

Jake dropped to the floor with the cover of the racks between him and the other man, twisting to keep from landing on his arm. Pounding down on his back, he slammed the wind out of himself.

The man behind the bar fired wildly, exploding cans above Jake, raining vegetables and thick peach syrup down on him.

"Fool," he growled. He should have shot the man when he came in the door, but he hadn't expected him to be there. A room out back, Miller had said.

Another shot blasted cans into the air, and Jake could hear the man muttering.

"Kill sumbitch. No sumbitch's gonna take me. Dropped my bottle—"

He was drunk. Pushing over onto his knees, Jake tried to get a better view between the cans. A slug ripped another off the shelf next to him and Jake dropped back down.

He could still hear the man talking. "M'on, you, m'on. Ole Rem's fought grizzlies and rattlesnakes with his bare hands.

Stomp a mudhole in anything, anybody—" Another shot. "M'on, damn you . . ."

"Fella," Jake called. "Listen, there's no reason for this. I don't want you. I just—"

More cans exploded. Jake crawled, one-handed, making his way to the end of the rack.

"Missed you once, ain't gonna do it 'gin—"

The hammer dropped on an empty chamber with a hollow snap.

Jake pushed his way up, coming around the rack. The bar was two shelves away from him now. A table of clothing, and more canned goods.

Behind the bar he could hear shells dropping on the floor.

"Fella—" Jake called.

No answer. Another shell rattled on the wood.

"Fella," Jake said, and came around the rack, bellying under the table of clothes. "Ain't no reason we have to—"

Above him, cans jumped, spewing into the air. Hugging the floor, beneath the table, Jake crawled forward, thumbing back the hammer on the Colt.

Slugs smashed the table wood above him, and knowing he had no choice, he rolled away from his arm, coming up on his feet, bolting upright, catching the table with his shoulders, exploding it backward.

Surprised, Rem stumbled back against the wall, his arm swinging the gun around in reflex.

Jake shot him square in the chest, ramming him further back into the bottles, smashing them; then put another an inch to the right of the first to finish the job, twisting the dying man around, smearing broken glass with blood as he raked across the wall, crashing through the bottles in an echo of shots, slamming to the wooden floor.

Trembling, Jake lowered his gun, and walking to the bar, he leaned against it. He suddenly felt very tired.

Behind him, he could hear the scraping of the door.

"Jake—" Miller called.

"Yeah, Ed," he answered. "We're finished, come on in."

Turning, he started for the door, as Miller came in.

The storekeeper's eyes roamed bewilderedly.

"Glad you fellas didn't know each other," he said.

"Yeah," Jake frowned, and turning, walked outside to the front porch and sat down heavily on a bench. He put the gun down beside him.

Out of the corner of his eye he saw Addie and Mrs. Miller come around the side of the building.

"Mr. Hooker," Addie swallowed, her voice trembling and thick.

"I'm still here," he answered quietly.

Miller came out of the store. "Another one to bury," he said to his wife.

Jake looked up. "Sorry," he said, and stood wearily. "Gonna have to leave you with all the work, Ed."

"You headed out now—"

"Have to," Jake nodded. "Need a fresh horse, some supplies." He looked at Addie. "And a place for her until you can take her down or somebody can come for her—"

Miller held up his hands. "Hold on a minute, Jake, you mind tellin' me what this is all about?"

"Those fellas robbed me. I want to catch 'em 'fore they get to Mexico—"

Miller's eyes narrowed. "Mexico? They ain't headed for Mexico."

Jake's eyes came around. "What?"

Miller shook his head. "Headed up toward the high country. Long's Meadow. Said they was supposed to meet a fella."

"Meet a fella?"

Miller nodded. "Name of Ballard."

Jake heard Addie's breath catch. "Papa . . ." she whispered.

Jake looked from the girl to Miller again, his eyes narrowing. "You sure, Ed?"

"As I can be about anything," Miller shrugged. "That was the name though, I'm sure of that."

"Jesus," the hunter whispered. "That's why they didn't come back. He was already on his way with the money—" He turned to Miller. "Let's find me a horse," he said. "A good one. And fast."

# TWENTY-FOUR

Jake disappeared around the side of the building with Miller and the roan, and Addie had a sudden impulse to follow him. Being without him seemed wrong somehow.

"I'll show you your room," Mrs. Miller said, and Addie followed her through the store. "Regular room's through there," the big woman chattered. "But I'll let you stay in my daughter's room. She's gone now and . . ." The woman kept talking but Addie wasn't really listening as they went off to one side into a large kitchen, then a sitting room, and through it to a small bedroom.

"Not much," Mrs. Miller said, smoothing the covers and brushing dust from the chifforobe, "but you'll be snug enough."

Addie walked to the window as the big woman went on talking. She watched Jake and Miller cross toward the corrals.

"Ain't often we have a young lady stay with us," Mrs. Miller sighed.

Addie pulled her eyes from the window. "Thank you." She forced a smile.

"Bet you'd like to wash up," Mrs. Miller said. "Best get you some water." Coming around the bed, she picked up the bowl and pitcher from the nightstand. "Now you make yourself comfortable," she said as she went through the door.

Addie turned back to the window.

Jake was pulling his saddle off the roan at the gate as Miller picked up a hackamore from the fence, then took a handful of oats from a sack at the gate, and walked toward a small broad-chested brown pony.

The horse nuzzled into the oats in Miller's hand and when the horse had eaten the last of them, Miller strung the hackamore around his neck and led him to Jake.

"Your water," Mrs. Miller said, coming back into the room and setting the bowl and pitcher down on the nightstand. "Wash up now. Make you feel better."

"Yes," Addie nodded. "Maybe it will."

"Always does," the big woman agreed, then glancing out the window, she shook her head. Miller was saddling the horse as Jake watched.

"Ole Jake," Mrs. Miller frowned. "Never knowed him to let anybody do his work for him. Prideful to the point of sin. Arm must be hurtin' him some."

"Yes," Addie nodded. "I think it is."

"Hope he can make it up those mountains alone," the big woman sighed.

Addie looked at her. "What's it like? Between here and Long's Meadow?"

Mrs. Miller frowned. "A hard ride," she said, then patted Addie on the shoulder. "But don't worry yourself about it." She turned toward the door. "I'll see to makin' you somethin' to eat. Sound good?"

"Yes," Addie nodded. "Thank you."

The big woman hurried out of the room and Addie's gaze returned to the window. Jake was leaning against the corral logs, holding his arm. He looked very tired and very old.

"Damn," she whispered, lifting her eyes to the mountains, then letting them fall back to the old hunter.

He was untying the saddlebags. Dragging them off the horse, he tried to get them to his shoulder and dropped them. Miller came around the horse and picked them up for him, and easing them over his shoulder, Jake came toward the store.

"Damn," she whispered again, her hand tightening into a fist against her stomach, fighting what she knew she was about to do.

It didn't make sense. She was safe.

Her eyes followed Jake as he came to the back of the store and inside.

She stared after him for a moment, then turned from the window, starting for the door.

There was something more to it now.

More than being safe.

Jake finished with his supplies in the store.

"If you'd start a bill for me, I'd appreciate it," he said to Mrs. Miller. Then he picked up the sack and saddlebags, resting them on his shoulder. "Where's the girl?"

"In our girl's room. Washin' up, I think."

Jake glanced at the door and shifted his weight uncomfortably. "Put these on the horse," he said. "Then say goodby to her."

Carrying the sack and saddlebags, he walked across the store and out the back.

Halfway to the corral he saw Miller saddling another horse.

"What . . . ?" he wondered, then saw Addie behind the horse, handing the storekeeper the cinch.

As Jake approached, Miller straightened and looked at him, shrugging a confused grin.

"Said she wanted a horse," he said.

"Thanks, Ed," Jake nodded. "I'll handle it."

"Yeah." Miller shook his head, and picking up his shovel, he walked to where he'd started digging a grave.

Addie was still behind her horse as Jake walked to the brown pony and strung the sack over the horn. Turning, he looked at the girl, even though he couldn't see her face behind the horse.

"What're you doin'?" he asked.

"I . . . I'm going with you," she said.

"You're what?"

She came around the horse. "I'm going with you."

"The hell you are."

"The hell I'm not—"

"You're stayin' here."

Addie's mouth hardened. "You're giving me orders again."

"Well, somebody has to," Jake exploded. "Goddammit, Miss Ballard, there ain't no reason for you to go on."

Her eyes fell. "Yes," she countered, her voice quiet. "There is."

"Why?"

She frowned reluctantly. "Because you can't make it on your own."

Jake stared at her, his eyes softening for a moment, then hardening again. "I don't want you along," he said, turning to his horse.

"I don't care what you want, Mr. Hooker."

Jake hesitated, looking back at her. "What the hell's got into you anyhow? Two days ago—"

"I don't know," she snapped frustratedly, then lowered her voice. "I guess nobody ever needed me before. You and my father."

"Your pa? I thought—"

"I know," she nodded. "But I can't just let him die," she said, and turning, walked to her horse and mounted him.

Jake watched her; then shaking his head, he went to his own horse and pulled himself clumsily into the saddle.

He looked at Addie again. "You know—" he began, then frowned. "Hell," he growled, and swung his horse around, shouting him out.

Addie stood still for a moment, then kicking her horse, she caught up with Jake.

# TWENTY-FIVE

Canfield and Gage made the summit above Long's Meadow just before nightfall.

Riding across the bald, wind-blown top to the edge, they dismounted and looked down. The mountain fell away from them into a rocky face of giant boulders, then to a sparse tree line. Beyond the trees, hovering in the half-light, Canfield could see the meadow.

Holding his hat, he knelt down and squinted into the twilight.

And nodded. Standing, he pointed to a dot of light on the meadow, then looked to Gage, and smiled.

"I told you he'd wait," he said.

Jake threaded his mount between low rock, leaning out of the saddle and trying to see in the coming darkness. The horse stumbled, jolting him forward. Grasping the saddle horn quickly, he managed to stay mounted. He pulled himself back up and reined the horse in. Looking into the night, he shook his head wearily.

"Are we stopping?" Addie asked.

"No," Jake answered. "Can't pick out the trail any more. Gonna have to hoof it."

"You mean you can see to track?"

"Well," he admitted, "not really. But now I know exactly where they're headed. Don't need their track, but I will have to walk to get through a lot of this ground."

"You're tired, Mr. Hooker. Perhaps if we rested awhile."

"No." He shook his head. "I figure they camped on the summit above the meadow. That's about where they would have made it to. Besides, there they've got a lookout on the whole country. Only chance we've got is comin' up on 'em in the night and gettin' the drop on 'em in the mornin'.'"

Addie nodded. "I'll do it then," she shrugged, and dismounted.

Jake watched her. "Miss Ballard," he protested. "You—"

"Why not? You can point the way, and I can lead the horses."

"Now look," he growled. "I ain't about to let a girl—"

"Will you listen to me for once? You're tired. You may not make it if you try to walk. You're going to have to let me do it." She picked up the reins. "Now shut up and let's get going," she ordered him, and turning, she started walking.

"Damn," he whispered, then smiled quietly. "Guess there is something lower'n ridin' behind a woman. Havin' one lead you like a kid ridin' a pony."

They moved out. Pulling up the slopes and riding, he looked up at the sky.

Only the stars and fluid vagueness of the mountains blending, turning. There would be no moon tonight.

Moving upward, Jake could feel the mountain chill gathering around him. They crossed a meadow, then passed through a park of trembling aspen. Dark flowers and dark leaves brushed him as he passed.

The rise toward the mountains was gradual, but it was there. The air became cooler, crystal, scented with pine and space.

They climbed upward. Into the curved, pale darkness.

Jake's eyes fell to the girl, walking. She was tired too, he knew, but she moved relentlessly. He didn't understand her. He probably never would. But the distance in her seemed gone. Her motion seemed to be his motion. Climbing. Walking. Bound for the high country. And in their portion of the darkness, they seemed to be the only things real.

They came out on a crest. The hill fell away from them into the night, rushing to blackness.

Addie stopped.

"Mr. Hooker—?"

"Yeah?"

"Which way?"

His eyes scanned the darkness. "There," he pointed along the crest.

Without saying anything, the girl started out again, following the line of the hill, down into a small hollow; then Jake directed her out of it, to a ridge line lifting upward.

The ridge steepened and a wind began to come up from below. Shivering, Jake gathered his coat around him. The ridge kept rising, pulling away from the lower hills and mountains, and coming over a small rise, the summit stood above them. A great shoulder of darkness in more darkness.

"Miss Ballard," Jake whispered, and the girl stopped, looking up at him.

"We're here," he said.

# TWENTY-SIX

Jake dismounted, and with Addie's help, he tied blankets around the horse's hoofs to quiet them, then led the animals up the ridge.

The wind battered across them as they came to where the ridge widened into the summit. Moving out onto the summit, they skirted along the edge, and made their way into a clump of rocks and out of the wind.

Addie hobbled the horses as Jake pulled the blankets from their feet; then they both sank into the rocks. Jake handed a blanket to the girl and turned his eyes across the summit, peering into the darkness. In the distance, he could make out a slight shadow of movement.

"Their horses," he nodded. "Right where I would have picked."

Pulling a blanket around him, he crouched down beside the girl.

"Why don't you go after them now?"

He glanced at her sideways. "Mind if I sit a minute before I get my rear shot off."

She frowned. "I didn't mean it that way. I just meant that they're probably asleep, and in the darkness—"

Jake nodded. "I know, I know. Sometimes you sure make me want to look for a dog to kick though." Lifting his good arm, he motioned in front of them. "This summit flattens some from the ridge we came up, then rises here. The way down is right over there down the slope, on the other side of Canfield. There's no cover up here except an outcropping near them, and the rock face that runs from down below here around under their camp to the way down. Now those

fellas are used to sleepin' with one eye cocked. I got caught
out there—with no cover, I'd be a dead man."

"What are you going to do?"

"Wait 'till mornin' and light. Get down in those rocks
along the face and make my way around to their camp. Let
'em mount up, then hit 'em on horseback. Man on a horse
has a harder time hittin' something than a man on solid
ground. The difference might make up for them bein' two,
and havin' those automatic pistols."

The girl frowned. "It just seems awfully dangerous."

Jake smiled. "It is," he nodded. "Now get some sleep."

They waited. Jake eased back against a rock, and Addie
lay down, pulling the blanket over her. She lay there for a
while, then sat up again.

"What's wrong?" Jake asked.

"Can't sleep."

Jake frowned. "Try harder," he said, and looked back
across the summit.

Addie sat for a moment, staring at Jake, then spoke hesitantly. "Mr. Hooker . . . ?"

"What?"

"Who is Angie?"

"My sister," he replied before he thought, then looked
at Addie. "How'd you—"

"Last night," Addie answered. "You talked in your sleep."

Frowning, he nodded.

"What happened to her, Mr. Hooker? And the rest of your
family? You talked about them too."

"They're dead," he said quietly.

"How?"

His eyes came around, looking at her. The only real form
he could see in the darkness.

"Please, Mr. Hooker, she pressed him. "I'd like to know."

"Why?"

"Because," she shrugged, her voice thick. "You're the nearest thing I've ever had to a . . . friend." She selected the word carefully. "And I'd like to know about you."

Jake nodded and felt a trembling in his chest as he remembered. "I was about eight," he began. "It was just after the war, and things were hard in Virginia. My pa was a Confederate, and like ever'body else that came home, he was broke. The only thing we had was a small farm. Pa got one crop out of it, then didn't get hardly nothin' for it. He sold the place and with the money he bought a Conestoga wagon. He packed me and Ma, my brother Ethan and sister Angie, into it and we started west." He swallowed, his voice becoming tighter. "We was just into Ohio when Angie come down with a fever, then started gettin' splotches on her face. Then me and my brother Ethan got it. I come out of it in a couple of days, and by then Ma and Pa had it too. Pa managed to get the wagon down by a river, just outside a town. I cared for 'em for a couple of days the best I could, but I was awful young, and they was awful sick. Nothin' I done seemed to do any good.

"Angie started gettin' worse, so I run into town and stopped at the first house. Told the man that my folks were sick. He and his wife come back with me, but when they seen it was the hard measles, they turned and got the hell out of there.

"I done what I could for Pa and Ma and Ethan and Angie, but on the morning of the third day, Angie died. Just all of a sudden she was still. Not movin'. I reckon I kinda went crazy, cause I shook her and yelled at her to get up, then went runnin' toward the town again.

"The man and his wife musta told the townsfolk about us, because there was a city marshal waitin' for me on the edge of town.

"He put a rifle on me and said I wasn't comin' in that town." Jake's jaw stiffened. "I begged that sonofabitch, but all he did was cock the hammer on the rifle and tell me to get out of there.

"I went back to the wagon. Ma and Ethan died a few

days later. Pa, he took a week." His hand gathered into a fist. "All that time . . . all that time nobody come from town. They let four people die . . ."

"There was probably nothing they could have done," Addie offered.

"They coulda helped," Jake growled, his fist trembling. "They coulda tried . . ."

"Yes," Addie agreed quietly, "they should have."

Jake eased his hand open. "After that I come west. Worked in stores and bars cleanin' out, then on a keel boat 'till I was thirteen and had me some money saved. Then I started trappin'. Stayin' to myself mostly. Found a valley in the Flathead country I always meant to settle in." He frowned. "But folks and their fences got there first. That's when I decided on this Australia. Heard they ain't got many towns or people there."

"They'll come," Addie said.

Jake's eyes eased around. "You're the second one to tell me that," he said, then looked away, staring into the darkness. "But it don't matter. I'm goin'. Come hell or high water, I'm goin'."

"I hope you make it," she said.

"I will," he nodded, then glanced back at her. "You know," he said. "That's the first time I told anybody all of it . . ." He pulled his eyes away. "Must be gettin' mushheaded," he sighed.

"Mr. Hooker—"

"Get some sleep," he interrupted her.

"But—"

"Good night, Miss Ballard," he said with a note of finality in his voice.

Nodding, she lay back.

"Good night," she said.

# TWENTY-SEVEN

Morning stirred. Wet, shadow-filled, blurring the night into form.

Stretching, Jake sat up. He hadn't allowed himself to sleep, but he felt refreshed. Ready. Easing himself to the edge of the rocks, he looked down the summit. He could see two forms in their blankets. The horses off to one side.

Turning, he touched Addie, nudging her awake.

Stirring, she pulled her blanket tighter, then opened her eyes.

Jake touched his lips to quiet her. "Morning," he whispered. "Gonna be leavin' in a minute."

Standing, he walked to their horses, took the saddlebags from his mount, and draped them over his shoulder. Then slipping the Winchester from its boot he went back to Addie.

Kneeling down, he handed her the rifle.

"You know how to use one of these?" he asked.

"Yes," she nodded. "I think so."

"Push down on that," he nodded at the lever, and she did. "And bring it back up. Now it's ready to fire. Just keep doin' that and you'll be all right."

She looked up at him, smiling wanly. "Sometimes I think I'm learning a profession."

Jake's eyes clouded. "In a way you are. Sorry."

She shook her head. "My choice."

Jake nodded gently, then took the saddlebags from his shoulder and laid them on the ground. Reaching inside, he took out a box of shells and put them in his coat pocket, then he lifted his pistol from its holster. Opening the gate, he rolled the cylinder until an empty chamber showed, then shifting the gun to his bad hand, he held it weakly and dropped in another shell. Taking it with his good hand again, he closed the chamber gate and put the gun back in its holster.

"Now I just hope I don't blow my leg off. Totin' a shell under the hammer ain't too wise. Then again if I had any sense I wouldn't be here."

He lifted his eyes to the girl.

"If somethin' happens," he said, "get on that horse and ride like hell."

He started to turn.

"Mr. Hooker—"

Hesitating, he looked back at her.

She swallowed. "Take care," she whispered.

A softness touched his lips, tugging at them. He nodded to her wordlessly, then pivoting, he rushed down the slope and into the rocks and darkness and was gone.

Walt Canfield stirred from his blankets, and sitting up pulling on his jacket, he heard something in the darkness.

Off toward the ridge, back down the way they'd come.

Reaching down, he drew his automatic and stood up, listening. Waiting.

The wind careened across the naked ground. There was no other sound.

Shrugging, he holstered the gun. "Imaginin' things," he sighed, and glanced down at Phil Gage's sleeping form.

Turning, he kicked the big man's boots. "You're burnin' daylight," he said.

Gage sat up blinking and began climbing out of his blankets. Canfield ambled toward the rock face and looked at the coming morning.

Darkness still drifted the soft void, but Canfield could make out the forming lines of ridges, mesas, and peaks beginning to fold out of one another.

The wind rushed up around him, carrying the quiet.

"Looks like you could see all the way to China, don't it," Gage said, coming up behind him.

Canfield smiled. "Other'n facin' the wrong direction, yeah," he nodded, and the smile softened. "Always liked the run of this country. Lot of it down in the Sierra Madre. Maybe get me a rancho down there. Big place with servants to bring me rum."

Gage grinned, sighing. "You're beginnin' to sound like Rem."

Canfield's eyes pulled up. "What?"

"You know all that blabberin' he does about his place—"

"Oh," Canfield nodded stiffly. "Yeah." He turned suddenly, walking back to the rolls. "Stupid idea." Picking up his saddle, he threw it on his horse.

"Ain't we gonna eat?"

"No time," Canfield said, tightening the cinch. "Now let's butt these saddles and pay Ballard a visit."

It was harder going in the rocks than Jake thought it would be. His broken arm was like carrying around a piece of dead throbbing lead, and it kept him off balance. He'd almost fallen once jumping from one rock to another. Now, crouching in the boulders, he looked ahead of him.

Mostly it was just steep and rough. A few scrub bushes.

Pushing himself up, he began threading his way through the rocks again. Down a space between giant building-sized boulders, then up again, coming close to the fall of the summit. Keeping low, he made his way on his good hand, then lying down, he looked out across the open space. He spotted the fire, then the shadows of the men.

He was a little behind them. And they were moving. From their horses to their rolls and back.

Jake shoved back down from the crest hurriedly, turning through the rocks. He was going to have to push it to make it in front of them.

Running, he came out on an overhang, leaped across to another tongue-like rock, charged down it, and around another boulder. The ground steeped under him and suddenly he was moving faster than he wanted, plunging through the half-light across shadowed granite and sandstone. Coming out onto a shelf, he saw space in front of him, and a drop, and looking to his right, he saw another smaller shelf leading upward. Jumping, he slammed down on the small shelf solidly, giving it his full weight, and as soon as he hit it, he felt it give under him, moaning. Still moving, he thrust his good hand up the wall above him, shoving his fingers into a crack in the sandstone as the flat rock dropped out from under him, crashing downward, slamming through the boulders, leaving him dangling in the darkness.

Pulling himself up into the saddle, Walt Canfield heard something from the rocky face. Rock slamming into rock. Heavy rock.

He looked to Gage. He had heard it too.

"Goat?" he ventured, but didn't believe it even as he said it.

"No," Canfield growled. "Somethin' bigger'n that. Takes weight to move a rock that size." Reaching down, he pulled his pistol.

"Walt," Gage snapped. "We can ride on. Maybe we can make it to the slope."

Canfield shook his head. "He's been behind me long enough," he growled, and spurring his horse, he ran for the rocks.

From the far side of the summit, Addie watched the two men mount their horses and hesitate. They were talking. Then Canfield pulled his pistol and was turning away from the slope down.

"Jake," she whispered. They must have seen or heard him.

They were riding back along the rock face.

Shoving the Winchester up, laying it out on a rock, she swallowed, grasped the handle through the lever, and

brought her finger back on the trigger, squeezing. The first
shot surprised her with the recoil slamming the butt back
into her shoulder, but pushing the rifle forward again, she
levered another shell into the chamber and fired again.

At the sound of the shots, Canfield hauled his horse in,
looking back around.

"What the—"

A slug blasted the dust in front of him, then another off
to one side.

Gage's horse crowhopped under him and he tore the animal's head around.

"The rocks," Canfield yelled, and they ran into chest-
high outcropping jutting up from the face of the cliff and
dismounted.

"Two of 'em," Gage guessed.

"Likely," Canfield agreed, then looked down into the
rocks of the face. "Keep that one there," he said. "I'm
going after the other one in the rocks."

"Let's get the hell out of here." Gage shook his head.

"No," Canfield growled. "Not this time."

And without waiting for Gage to say anything Canfield
was up, running past the horses and into the rocks.

Below Canfield and Gage, his good hand still gripping
the crack in the rock, Jake heard the firing.

Addie, he thought. She had bought him a few minutes.

He looked up. There was nowhere to go there. Besides,
with one arm, he wasn't going to be doing a lot of climbing. His eyes slipped downward over the rock. He was lying
on a slight incline, and the pull on his grip wasn't too bad,
but he couldn't stay there long.

His eyes searched the darkness. Below him, a few feet
away, was the rest of the ledge he'd knocked away. Turning
over on his back, and stretching his legs out, Jake swung
himself around, throwing his foot. He missed. Twisting, he
slumped over on his back again. His breath ached through

him, and his hand was beginning to cramp. He had to move again. Fast.

He stretched his legs apart. Lifting. Swinging. Throwing the foot out. And caught the tip of the ledge.

He held himself steady for a moment, then eased his weight down on the foot. Balancing himself, he loosened his grip slightly, and scraped his hand along the crack. More pressure on the foot. He pushed his hand, until he was straightened on the ledge, then slipped his other foot to it.

Crouching down for a moment, he rested, squeezing the sweat out of his eyes. Gravel rattled down on him from above and he could make out the slight whisper of footfalls. His eyes jerked up and he stood, lifting his Colt from his belt, listening.

There was more rifle fire from above. Small punctures in the wind. It was the Winchester. Addie was still firing.

"Good girl," he murmured, and trembling, he strained to pick out the direction of the footfalls in the gravel, but the wind blurred them away. Whoever it was, Canfield or both of them, was likely staying to the solid rock now.

Jake eased out. Down the ledge. Threading into the twisting sandstone. The wind increased, blurring the vague sunlight with dust, mingling in the boulders, making everything half, gnarling the jagged shapes of the rocks and bushes into something misshapen.

Slipping back toward the crest, he came up into an arch formed by two building-sized boulders. There was a passage between them, head-high, dark, bent upward like a warped hallway. Above him at the other end Jake could see an open space. Dust exploded by the wind blasted down it.

Pressing into the archway, Jake was halfway up the tunnel when a form filled the opening above, darkening the sun. Without thinking, Jake dove backward, twisting into the dirt, slamming down on his arm, screaming as he fell. He only half heard the fire from the automatic as it ripped over the ground where he'd been standing.

Still screaming, Jake tumbled down the incline and

through the passage. Above him, Canfield charged into the entrance, blasting the roof and walls of the tunnel as Jake plummeted through the opposite end and into the open, sprawling in the dirt.

The white-hot pain in his arm and the firing seemed to be the same thing for a moment. More shots raked through the stone tunnel, the sound roaring down on him.

Gathering strength in his water-like legs, Jake jacked them under him, then pushed, hurling himself off to the side and out of the opening.

A line of dirt spasmed where he'd been lying. Then again. Dragging the Colt, Jake thumbed two shots into the archway, then shoved himself up, rolling on his back down a boulder, dropping on the lower side.

He started to get up, but the pain in his arm thickened behind his eyes and he nearly passed out. He slumped to his knees. Above him, he heard more shots spray out of the arch in a wash of sound. He had to move. His good hand reached out in reflex, and fighting the pain, he crawled. Scraping along the rock, back upward, he came along the side of one of the boulders forming the arch, and hesitated, listening.

The wind exploded around Jake, stealing sound, isolating him in screaming silence.

Trembling against the pain in his arm, he heard the pop of Addie's shots above him again, mixing with the whinny of horses.

Straightening, he started into the rocks below him, then hearing the horses again, he stood and looked back up toward the summit.

And smiled.

The horses.

If he could get to them he could make sure Canfield wouldn't get away again.

Turning quickly, he ran up the giant boulder, over the top of the arch, across the crack to the adjoining boulder, then down it a short way to the slope and into more cover.

Keeping low, he threaded his way upward through the labyrinth of sandstone.

The summit came into view slowly. There were still a lot of rocks between them but he could make out the bobbing of the horses' heads. Crouching, he moved upward, then eased up a low rock for another look.

The horses were slightly into the outcropping, he could make that out, but he still couldn't see the man he figured was still with them.

"Damn," he grumbled to himself, and was turning when the ground below him exploded. Tumbling, he pushed himself over the opposite side of the sandstone as the swarm of slugs lashed up it, then pounded the boulders beyond Jake.

His arm throbbing, Jake pressed down into the dirt as another shock of fire tore holes in the rock above him.

Then stopped.

Jake looked up, and straining his ears, he heard the snap of metal on metal.

The man below him had shot dry.

Jake moved. Pushing up. Running half on his good hand and knees at first, then scrambling across a small clearing and up into a sink of sandstone, making for the horses.

"Gage," the man below him called. "He's comin' toward you."

Raising up, Jake pumped three shots downslope toward the voice; then turning, ran again, cutting for the horses, weaving, crawling, then running again. The man with the horses began firing, and Jake slipped downslope a little, then doubled back, turning toward the summit.

He came out with the open ground on one side and the outcropping on the other. Keeping the rocks between him and the two men, he knelt down to check his gun. Opening the chamber gate with his thumb, he rolled the cylinder over his leg. There was one cartridge left.

"Dammit," he growled, and sat down. Pulling his legs up toward his chest, and pressing them together, Jake wedged the Colt down between his knees. Holding it there, he tugged cartridges from his coat pocket and laid them in his lap. Then, picking up a shell, he slipped it into the chamber, rolled the cylinder and put another in. He repeated the maddeningly slow process until the gun was loaded.

Sighing his relief, he closed the chamber gate and took the gun back in his good hand then eased himself up a little.

The wind blasted over him, and looking across the summit, he saw a slight movement of color where Addie was hiding.

A horse's nicker, like a sliver in the wind, jerked his eyes around and he moved out, pushing around the boulders, letting the pistol lead him.

Ahead of him, he could make out movement. A horse's head bobbing.

Cocking the hammer of the Colt, he was starting around a rock, when something slashed through the flesh of his thigh, twisting him around, sending him tumbling into the rocks.

Across the summit, Addie had been watching Jake as he inched his way around the outcropping toward the horses, then saw him suddenly slammed around, falling as the muffled thump of the shot blurred through the wind.

He seemed to fall for a long time in nightmare movement, sprawling.

She stood up slowly, the rifle slipping from her hands. "Jake," she whispered, and without thinking about it, she was running.

Coming up through the outcropping of the rim, Canfield heard Gage's shots, then the scream.

"Gage," he called.

"I got him," was the answer.

Smiling, Canfield ran through the boulders and out between Gage and where he'd heard the man scream.

Gage came up behind him.

"There," he pointed into the rocks a few feet away.

Nodding, Canfield thumbed the hammer and turned, raising the pistol, when a movement off to the side pulled his eyes around.

Pivoting, he saw a figure break from the rocks across the summit. A small man it looked like at first, then he saw the blond hair blossom from under the hat as it blew away.

The Ballard girl.

Frowning, he swung the blunt-nosed pistol up.

Gage watched the motion, unbelieving for a moment. "Walt—" he barked.

"Shoulda done this at the beginning," the leader said, still lifting the gun, leveling it, and drawing a bead on the girl.

"Walt—"

Canfield's finger tightened on the trigger. The girl was still running.

"Walt," Gage whispered, then screamed. "Goddammit, I ain't gonna kill women," he raged, and charged Canfield.

Surprised, Canfield reeled, trying to bring the gun around; but Gage hit him first, catching his gun hand, and ducking a shoulder, plowing into Canfield, sending them both tumbling back into the dirt.

In the rocks, lying on the ground, half dazed, Jake heard the commotion and looked up to see the two men rolling on the ground, fighting.

Must have passed out for a minute, Jake thought; then starting to move, he felt the pain from his leg. Wincing, he looked down at it, then put a little weight on it. At least it wasn't busted too, he observed, and pushing himself up, he could see the men better now.

And someone beyond them, running.

"Addie," he whispered, and picking up his gun, he pulled himself up on a rock.

The girl came around the men to him.

"Get down," Jake snapped, grabbing her hand, hauling her around behind him.

On the ground, Canfield fought to get free of the big

man on top of him. Gage's hand was still fixed on the wrist of Canfield's gun hand. Twisting it, trying to break it.

Under him, Canfield could feel the bone about to give. Wrenching around, he pulled his feet between him and the big man, then straightened his legs, thrusting Gage back, throwing him sprawling to the ground.

Canfield clamored to his knees, bringing the pistol up.

Turning in the dirt, Gage saw what was coming. He almost looked glad.

Without hesitation, Canfield shot the big man twice, kicking him around like a huge, badly made rag doll, dead when he hit the ground.

It was quiet for a moment. Motionless. Only the wind ripping across the rocks and ground and people. Objects foreign to its flux.

In the rocks, Jake moved a second before Canfield did. Lifting his gun.

Canfield's shoulder shifted to turn.

"Don't," Jake warned him.

Nodding, the man on the ground let his pistol ease into the dirt, then he brought his eyes around, studying Jake.

"I don't even know you," he finally said. "What the hell do you want?"

"I was back at the stage stop," Jake answered. "You took some money from me."

Canfield's eyes narrowed at him, trying to recognize him; then shaking his head, he laughed wearily.

"As simple as that," he sighed.

"The money," Jake said.

"Yeah," Canfield nodded. "The money." Pushing himself up to his feet, he faced Jake. "Mind if I reach in my pocket?"

Jake leveled the gun at him. "I don't mind at all."

Smiling, ruefully, Canfield eased his hand into his shirt pocket and tugged out the roll of bills, the rawhide still around it.

His eyes raised from the money to Jake.

"Don't suppose we could call it even? Give you your money. I can still be where I need to be."

"To meet her daddy?"

Canfield shrugged. "None of your concern."

Jake frowned. "That's true. But that money is. Hand it to me. Easy."

Canfield nodded. "Is a little windy, ain't it?" Bringing both hands up, he slipped off the rawhide holding it, and his eyes came up to Jake's. "Windy as hell, come to think of it . . ."

Jake lifted the gun.

Canfield shook his head. "I wouldn't," he cautioned Jake quietly, then smiled. "I figure I just found my edge." He glanced around. "You know, if I was to let go of this, it'd scatter all the way to Santa Fe. Maybe a little further." His eyes slipped back to Jake's. The smile faded. "Now I'm goin' down. I'll leave your money there."

"I take it I'll have to take your word on that."

Canfield's eyes hardened. "It's the best you're gonna do today," he said, and leaned down toward his gun. "Two fingers," he said, reaching down with his thumb and forefinger, lifting the .45 by the end of the handle and slipping it into his holster. Then he backed toward the horses, the money held out at arm's length.

Behind him, Jake could feel Addie, her eyes following Canfield.

"Mr. Hooker," she whispered.

Canfield still moved toward the horses, taking each step carefully.

"Mr. Hooker," Addie said again, her voice taut, and her hand touched his arm.

Jake trembled. He had come full circle. Only now it was him listening to somebody asking for help.

Swallowing, Jake began raising the gun, and limped around the rock holding him up.

"Canfield," he called quietly.

"I win this hand," Canfield replied, and turned, putting his back to Jake.

Jake watched him. And the money.

The gun was heavy in his hand.

Canfield neared the outcropping, lifting his hand for one of the horses.

"Dammit," Jake growled, and stepped forward, pushing away from the rock. Then shouted, "Canfield!"

The walking man reeled, his hand dropping for his gun.

Jake shot him as he turned. The first slug smashed his side, throwing him off balance. The second crushed his chest like rotten wood, slamming him backward. His hands floated up as he fell, the gun tipping out of his hand, the money exploding from him. Caught by the wind. A sudden shock of green. Fluttering like a thousand frail birds. Gone by the time Canfield slumped into the dirt.

Jake stared at him, then at the money still soaring, and he sat down wearily in the dirt, his eyes following the paper in the wind.

"Damn," he sighed.

Gravel crunched beside him and Addie sat down next to him, watching the money too.

"My God," she whispered.

"Hellava note, ain't it," Jake said.

They sat in silence as the last of the money blended into the air, disappearing.

"Your money—" Addie forced herself to speak.

A slow smile pushed through Jake's lips. "Pike was right." He cocked his head. "Never shoulda trusted that government paper." His smile faded. "He was right about some other things too."

"Aren't you going to try and go after it?"

Jake shook his head. "I been runnin' too long. Time I learned different."

"But that was all you had."

Jake looked at her. "No," he said, "It ain't. Not by a long shot."

Addie brought her eyes around. "Why did you do it, Mr. Hooker? You don't even know my father."

"That's right," he said, "I don't know him." He held his hand out. "Help me up," he asked.

Taking his arm, Addie managed to get him on his feet.

"Guess I—"

"Why?" she cut in. "Why did you do it, Mr. Hooker?"

Jake's eyes came around, a softness in his gaze.

"You—" he began, then blinking, he turned away. "Better see to the horses," he said, and began limping toward them.

Addie watched him, still feeling what had been in his eyes. And she realized that without meaning to, he had told why he'd done it.

For her.

Swallowing, she ran and caught up with him. She put his arm over her shoulder.

"What're you doin'?" he snapped.

"What does it look like? I'm helping you. Going to get you home where I can take care of you—"

"The hell you are—"

"Shut up."

He shook his head. "Damned if you're not gettin' more stubborn."

Her eyes lifted to his face, "I had a good teacher," she said.

Jake hesitated, looking down at her, then smiled. "So did I," he nodded, then sniffed. "But that don't mean I'm gonna let anybody stick me in no bed."

"You stubborn sonofabitch—"

"And that's another thing, you better start watchin' your language—"

"Don't tell me what to do—"

Arguing, they walked across the summit to their horses.

FIC Ham          Hammonds,
A gathering of wolves /
ATH  AF    1st ed.          1975.

Athens Regional Library System

3 3207 00120 0692

Waso
Brooks